DEATH IN THE TUNNEL

MILES BURTON

With an Introduction by

MARTIN EDWARDS

This edition published 2016 by
The British Library
96 Euston Road
London NW1 2DB

Originally published in 1936 by Collins

Cataloguing in Publication Data
A catalogue record for this book is
available from the British Library

ISBN 978 0 7123 5641 1

Text designed and typeset by Tetragon, London

Printed and bound by
TJ International Ltd, Padstow, Cornwall

DEATH IN THE TUNNEL

INTRODUCTION

Death in the Tunnel is a clever example of a popular branch-line of crime fiction, the "railway murder mystery". The book was originally published in 1936, just two years after the appearance of that legendary story of crime on a train, Agatha Christie's *Murder on the Orient Express*. The author, Miles Burton, was a friend of Christie's, but although he enjoyed considerable success in his day, his fame never came close to matching hers. *Death in the Tunnel* has long been out of print, with the result that it became highly sought-after by collectors.

In the first chapter, the body of Sir Wilfred Saxonby is found in a first-class compartment of the 5 p.m. train from London's Cannon Street to Stourford. He has been shot, and initial indications suggest that he has committed suicide while the train was passing through a long tunnel. Yet there is no apparent reason why he should wish to do away with himself, and a strange incident, when a mysterious red light in the tunnel caused the driver to slow down for a few moments, arouses the curiosity of Inspector Arnold of Scotland Yard. Arnold is a hard-working detective, "nothing if not methodical", but finding himself stumped by the puzzle, he consults his friend Desmond Merrion, a wealthy amateur in criminology.

Merrion, a highly imaginative chap, quickly comes up with the "essential brainwave" which helps to establish how Sir Wilfred met his end, but although it seems that the dead man fell victim to a complex conspiracy, the investigators are puzzled about the conspirators' motives, as well as their identities. Can there be a connection with Sir Wilfred's seemingly untroubled family life, his highly successful business, or his high-handed and unforgiving personality? And what is the significance of the wallet found on the corpse, and the bank notes that it contained? The trail leads Arnold to a former employee of Sir Wilfred's company, but Merrion eventually forms the view that the case will only be solved if an apparently cast-iron alibi can be cracked.

This is a story where the focus is on howdunit and whodunit, rather than on the characters' motivations. Miles Burton, unlike some of his contemporaries, had little interest in exploring criminal psychology, and this lack of interest in *why* his characters are driven to behave as they do is one reason why his work dropped out of sight after his death. But he had a meticulous way with plots, and this book (re-titled *Dark is the Tunnel* for the US market) received good reviews on both sides of the Atlantic.

"Torquemada" of the *Observer*, who along with Dorothy L. Sayers was one of the leading reviewers of detective fiction in the Thirties, reckoned the novel was Burton's best. In the Seventies, however, when books of this sort were deeply unfashionable, H.R.F. Keating published a short, light-hearted discussion of them, *Murder Must Appetize*, which teasingly highlights *Death in the Tunnel* for its less than spell-binding opening paragraph. The reader does not, however, have to wait many more paragraphs for death to darken that tunnel, and Keating, an instinctively generous commentator, conceded that the plot was "devilishly ingenious".

Miles Burton was one of the pen-names used by Cecil John Street (1884–1965), one of the most industrious of all detective fiction novelists. After publishing several factual books, Street launched his career as a crime writer with a thriller published under the rather transparent pseudonym John Rhode. His most famous detective, the cerebral Dr Lancelot Priestley, made his debut in *The Paddington Mystery* in 1925.

Five years later, Street became a founder member of the elitist Detection Club, formed by Anthony Berkeley. An affable man, Street formed strong friendships with fellow members such as Dorothy L. Sayers (who acknowledged his help with her description of a Playfair cipher in *Have His Carcase*), Lucy Malleson (who wrote under the pen-names Anthony Gilbert and Anne Meredith, and dedicated her autobiography to him) and the American specialist in "locked room" murder mysteries, John Dickson Carr, also known as Carter Dickson. He and Carr wrote one novel in collaboration together; this was *Drop to His Death*, re-titled *Fatal Descent* for the US market. Street also edited the transcript of the trial of Constance Kent (the case made famous in recent years by Kate Summerscale's *The Suspicions of Mr Whicher*) and compiled an anthology of work by Detection Club members, *Detection Medley*.

He continued to publish crime novels until the Sixties, but even his later work belonged in spirit to the "Golden Age of Murder" between the two world wars. For many years, his books were out of vogue, although his name—or rather his pen-names—were kept alive by *aficionados* willing to pay high prices for first edition copies of his novels. Some titles fetch thousands, rather than hundreds, of pounds if the book and its dust jacket are in first class condition. The rather more affordable titles in the British Library's Crime Classics series allow a new generation of readers a chance to deduce why the work of Street in his various incarnations has long commanded enthusiasm among lovers of traditional detective fiction.

MARTIN EDWARDS
www.martinedwardsbooks.com

SELECT BIBLIOGRAPHY:
Miles Burton and Golden Age detective fiction

J. Barzun and W.H. Taylor, *A Catalogue of Crime* (1971)
H.R.F. Keating, *Murder Must Appetize* (1975)
J. Barzun and W.H. Taylor, *A Book of Prefaces to Fifty Classics of Crime Fiction, 1900–1950* (1976)
Charles Shibuk, "John Rhode", in *Dictionary of Literary Biography, volume 77: British Mystery Writers 1920–39* (1989)
John Cooper and B.A. Pike, *Detective Fiction: the Collector's Guide* (2nd edn, 1994)
John Cooper and B.A. Pike, *Artists in Crime* (1995)
Melvyn Barnes, "John Rhode", in *St James Guide to Crime and Mystery Writers* (1996)
Curtis Evans, *Masters of the "Humdrum" Mystery: Cecil John Charles Street, Freeman Wills Crofts, Alfred Walter Stewart and the British Detective Novel, 1920–61* (2012)
Martin Edwards, *The Golden Age of Murder* (2015)

I

THE 5.0 P.M. TRAIN FROM CANNON STREET RUNS FAST AS FAR as Stourford, where it is due at 6.7. On Thursday, November 14th, it was, as usual, fairly full, but not uncomfortably so.

It was a fine evening, dark, but with no suggestion of fog. Drawn by a powerful locomotive of the Lord Nelson type, the train kept well up to schedule time. In fact it ran through Blackdown station at 5.29, two minutes earlier than it was timed to do.

Beyond the station is Blackdown Tunnel, two and a half miles long. The gradient through the tunnel is fairly severe, and the speed of the train slackened slightly as it entered it. Still, it must have been travelling at fully fifty miles an hour. Suddenly, about half-way through the tunnel, the brakes were violently applied. So violently that William Turner, the guard, was nearly thrown off his seat in the rear van.

His first thought was that the communication cord had been pulled. But on glancing at the vacuum brake apparatus in his van he saw this had not been the case. He left the van, and started along the corridor towards the front of the train, looking into each compartment as he passed. Nearly every seat in the long row of thirds was occupied, but none of the passengers seemed in any way concerned by the slowing up of the train, which was now rapidly coming to a stop.

Turner unlocked the door leading to the first-class compartments. Here, too, all was well. The firsts were not so densely populated as the thirds, but they contained a fair sprinkling of passengers, mostly reading their evening papers. As Turner passed up the corridor, he heard a whistle from the engine. The train, which had slowed down nearly to walking pace, began once more to gather way. Still, it was curious. Turner continued on his way, expecting to meet his assistant from the front end of the train, who might be able to tell him what had been the matter.

He reached the last of the first-class compartments, a smoker, and looked in. Yes, there was the old chap who had given him a quid to keep him a compartment to himself. The application of the brakes had not disturbed him. He had dozed off, with his glasses on his nose, and his paper on his knees. Some big toff, no doubt. Turner remembered having seen him on the line before.

The guard unlocked a second door, separating the firsts in the centre of the train from another row of thirds, in front of them. Just beyond it, he met his assistant, who had walked down the train from the front van. "What's up, Ted?" he asked.

"Everything O.K. my end," replied the other. "I thought Bert must have run over somebody, or something. But he's pushing her along again now, so it can't have been that. Perhaps he dropped a sixpence off the engine, and wanted to go back and look for it."

They exchanged a few more words, then each returned to his own van. Two or three minutes had been lost on schedule by the slowing down and gathering speed again. But this lost time was made good without difficulty. As the train approached Stourford, Turner noticed that the hands of his watch were barely past six o'clock. They would be well on time.

Once more he walked up the train, until he reached the first-class compartment occupied by the big toff, as he mentally styled him. The old gentleman was still asleep, and in the same position, as though he had not stirred since Blackdown Tunnel. Turner unlocked the door between the compartment and the corridor, and slid it back. "Just running into Stourford, sir!" he said loudly but respectfully.

The passenger did not move. So utterly still was he that Turner felt a sudden misgiving. He entered the compartment and laid his hand on the old gentleman's shoulder. This having no effect, he shook him gently. To his horror, the passenger swayed, and appeared to lose his balance. He fell sideways, and subsided uneasily across the arm-rest. Turner, who had been through a course of first-aid, felt his pulse, but could detect no beating. He loosened his collar, and set him in an easier position.

By this time the train was running into the station. Turner went back to the corridor, which in this particular coach was on the left-hand side, opened the window, and put his head out. The station-master was standing on the platform. As the train drew slowly past him, Turner spoke. "I'd like a word with you, Mr. Cutbush," he said quietly.

The station-master opened the door, and swung himself on to the train. "What is it?" he asked.

"There's a passenger in here I don't like the look of," replied Turner. "He was all right when we left Cannon Street, but he's pretty dicky now, I'm afraid."

The station-master entered the compartment. "Hallo, it's Sir Wilfred Saxonby, from Helverden!" he exclaimed. "He went up by the 9.50 this morning, and his car is in the yard now to meet him. Whatever can be the matter with him, I wonder?" As he spoke, the station-master unbuttoned the passenger's overcoat, and opened it out. He started back in horror. On the breast of the dark grey suit beneath it was a patch of wet blood.

Mr. Cutbush was fully equal to the emergency. He wasted no more time in fruitless examination of the body. "Slip out and send a couple of chaps for the stretcher, and then come back here and help get him into the waiting-room. We'll take this coach off here, and I'll take the names and addresses of the passengers in it. And when you've got Sir Wilfred into the waiting-room, slip into the booking-office and tell the clerk to ring up Dr. Frant."

Turner carried out his instructions to the letter. The body was removed from the train, and carried into the waiting-room, at the door of which a porter took up his post to keep out the inquisitive. The booking clerk was instructed to ring up Dr. Frant. Then Turner walked along the platform to the engine. "We're going to take off a first-class coach here, Bert," he said.

"All right," replied the engine-driver. "What's up? Hot box, or something?"

"No. The coach is all right, but there's a toff in it who must have committed suicide. Mr. Cutbush knows him. Sir Wilfred Somebody. He said we were to take the coach off. Thinks the police will want to have a look at it, I expect. By the way, what was wrong with you to pull up in the tunnel like that?"

"There wasn't anything wrong with me. Chap working on the line showed a red light. Then, just as I got to him, he turned it to green. So I came on."

"Chap working on the line!" Turner exclaimed. "There's nothing in the notices about any chaps working in Blackdown Tunnel!"

"I know that. But there was them blinking lights. You ask Charlie. He saw them, just the same as I did."

The fireman, who was leaning out of the cab, nodded. "Yes, I saw them," he said. "Chap was swinging them backwards and forwards, low down, just clear of the rails."

"Well, I'll have to put it in my report, I suppose," said Turner. "I'll get along now and see to the uncoupling of that coach."

The coach was removed and shunted into a siding, where all the windows were closed and the doors locked. The train continued on its journey. At twenty minutes past six, Dr. Frant arrived at the station, where he was shown into the waiting-room by Mr. Cutbush.

A very brief inspection served to show that Sir Wilfred Saxonby was dead. "Not very long, hardly an hour, I should imagine," said the doctor. "Now, let's see if we can find out what he died of. Just help me to undo his coat and waistcoat, and we'll see where that blood came from."

The cause of death was soon apparent. Upon Sir Wilfred's chest being bared, a small wound, surrounded with blood, was found in the region of the heart. A similar wound, but a trifle larger, was found in the back. The two wounds were level, that is to say that had the body been in an upright position, they would have been the same height above the ground.

"H'm!" said the doctor. "Pierced clean through the heart. By a bullet, I should say, though it might have been a very fine stiletto. Let's have a look at his overcoat."

Even in the not very powerful light of the waiting-room, the doctor found what he was looking for. "Here you are!" he exclaimed. "There's a very small hole, corresponding with the position of the wound. And round it you can see some black specks, where the cloth has been burnt. Those specks were made by burning grains of powder. Sir Wilfred was shot with a pistol of some kind, probably a very small automatic, fired at very short range. Has the compartment in which he was found been searched?"

The station-master shook his head. "I'm a servant of the railway company, doctor, not a policeman," he replied. "Every man to his trade, say I."

"Well, perhaps you're right," said Dr. Frant. "The police will want to look into this, and they'll be glad to find things undisturbed. It's a bad job, altogether. You realise, I suppose, that this wound could have been self-inflicted?"

Mr. Cutbush nodded. "Sir Wilfred was alone in the compartment, so the guard informs me," he said.

"Well, the best thing you can do is to get in touch with the police at once. I'll make arrangements for the body to be taken to the mortuary. There's nothing more I can do here, I'm afraid."

It was not long before the police, in the person of Inspector Marden, of the local constabulary, arrived on the scene. As the result of Marden's investigations, it was decided to call in the help of Scotland Yard. Not that there was much doubt as to what had happened, but it was just as well to make sure.

II

INSPECTOR ARNOLD, OF THE CRIMINAL INVESTIGATION Department, arrived at Stourford early on the following morning. He was met by Marden, who gave him a brief statement of the facts. "I don't think there's any doubt that it's a case of suicide," he said. "But the dead man is a pretty important person in these parts, and my chief is very anxious that everything should be done to clear the matter up. Shall we have a look round the compartment in which the body was found?"

"Hold on a minute," Arnold replied. "I'd like a little more information first. Who was this man, Sir Wilfred Saxonby?"

"A big man locally. Chairman of the bench of magistrates, and that sort of thing. He lived at Mavis Court, a big place near Helverden, about five miles from here. Lady Saxonby died some years ago. Sir Wilfred had a son and a daughter, but they are both married, and don't live at Mavis Court. Since Lady Saxonby's death Miss Olivia Saxonby, Sir Wilfred's niece, has kept house for him. Sir Wilfred was chairman of a firm with offices in the City somewhere, and used to go up to London once a week or so."

Arnold nodded. "Good enough. That'll do to go on with. Now I'm ready to have a look at that railway carriage of yours."

They summoned the station-master from his office; and the three of them walked across the metals to the siding on which stood the disconnected coach. It was nearly new stock, built of steel, a corridor coach of eight first-class compartments, with a lavatory at each end.

Mr. Cutbush produced a railway key, and unlocked one of the doors on the corridor side. They hoisted themselves into the coach, and Marden led the way to one of the end compartments. "This is the place," he said. "Now then, Mr. Cutbush, perhaps you'll be good enough to tell this gentleman where Sir Wilfred was sitting when the train came in."

"The coach was running with the corridor on the left-hand side, facing in the direction in which the train was moving," said the station-master. "This, then, was the front compartment in the coach. Sir Wilfred was in the corner seat, farthest from the corridor, with his back to the engine. None of the other five seats were occupied. The train runs fast from Cannon Street to here. After Sir Wilfred's body had been removed, I cleared everybody else out of the coach, taking their names and addresses as I did so. There were twenty-four other passengers in it. I then locked the coach up securely, and had it shunted to where it stands now."

"Mr. Cutbush and I examined it at seven o'clock yesterday evening," said Marden. "I had Dr. Frant's report, and the first thing I looked for was a bullet-hole in the back of the seat. Well, look here!"

He pointed out a small puncture in the upholstery, so small as to be hardly noticeable. "That's just about the size of the holes in Sir Wilfred's clothing," he said. "They are all about a quarter of an inch, not more."

"What is there behind this upholstery, Mr. Cutbush?" Arnold asked.

"A steel partition dividing this compartment from the lavatory," the station-master replied.

"Let's have a look in the lavatory," Arnold suggested. They examined the wall there, but there was no sign of a bullet-hole. "The steel partition stopped it, no doubt," Arnold continued. "We shall have to strip the upholstery in the compartment if we're to find it. Now what about the weapon it was fired from?"

"We found that, too," Marden replied. "If you'll come back to the compartment, I'll show you. I've put it back exactly where it was."

Arnold saw it for himself as soon as he examined the floor. It was lying under the seat which had been occupied by Sir Wilfred, only a few inches back from the front edge of the seat. Arnold picked it up and examined it. It was a miniature automatic pistol, of foreign make. The barrel was foul, and the magazine contained cartridges. On the butt was engraved a monogram which Arnold deciphered as "W.S."

"Had Sir Wilfred a firearms certificate in which this pistol was described?" Arnold asked.

"No, he hadn't," Marden replied. "I thought of that at once. He had a certificate for a revolver and a rifle, but not for an automatic pistol."

"That's queer," said Arnold. "I don't profess to be a firearms expert, but any one can see that this pistol is nearly brand new. Now, Sir Wilfred cannot have bought it in England without first obtaining a certificate. Was he in the habit of going abroad at all?"

"I believe so," Marden replied. "But you'd better ask Miss Saxonby."

In the rack above the seat occupied by Sir Wilfred was a small leather attaché-case. This also bore the initials W.S. Arnold tried the fastenings, but the case was locked. "Any other luggage?" he asked.

"No, Sir Wilfred had only been up to London for the day," replied the station-master. "He left here by the 9.50 yesterday morning, and was carrying that case then."

The only other objects in the compartment were two newspapers, the *Evening Standard* and the *Evening News*, both of the previous day's date. They had both been opened.

"One of them was lying on the seat next to Sir Wilfred," said Mr. Cutbush. "The other was on the floor when I saw it, but the guard, William Turner, says that it was on Sir Wilfred's knee, and that it fell off when he tried to rouse him. Inspector Marden asked me to arrange to have Turner here this morning. He ought to have arrived by now. You can see him in my office, if you like."

Since there was nothing more to be seen in the compartment, they locked it once more, and went to the station-master's office. Mr. Cutbush ascertained that Turner had arrived, and sent for him. "Well, Turner, what can you tell us about this business?" Arnold asked.

"I can't tell you much, sir, and that's a fact," the guard replied. "The dead gentleman came up to me as I was standing on the platform at Cannon Street, about seven or eight minutes before the five o'clock was due to go out. I'd seen him before, travelling up and down, but I didn't know then who he was. 'Are you the guard of this train?' he says. 'Yes, sir, that's right,' says I. 'Well, I want you to find me a first-class carriage to myself as far as Stourford,' he says. And with that he slips a quid-note into my hand."

"What, a pound note!" Arnold exclaimed. "Passengers don't often give you pound notes to keep them carriages to themselves, do they?"

Turner's eyes twinkled. "Well, sir, that depends. I won't say but that now and then a young couple that don't want to be disturbed might slip a note into my hand. But they like coaches with no corridors, mostly. I don't mind that a gentleman like Sir Wilfred has given me a quid before.

"Well, I walks up the train with him, and looks into the first-class compartments. There was somebody in every one of them until we came to the last, the front one of the coach, if you understand me, sir. I put Sir Wilfred into that, and he took the seat farthest from the platform with his back to the engine. Then, since the corridor side of the coach was next to the platform, I locked the door between the compartment and the corridor. I didn't worry about the other door of the compartment, since there was a blank wall that side of the line, and nobody couldn't get in that side."

"So that, when the train started, the door of the compartment leading into the corridor was locked, and the door on the other side unlocked?"

"That's right, sir. And that's how they were until just before we ran into Stourford. And then I went along to unlock the door, seeing that that was the side the gentleman would have to get out."

"Did you see Sir Wilfred during the journey from Cannon Street to Stourford?"

"Yes, sir. I saw him while we was running through Blackdown Tunnel, after the check."

"After the check?" Arnold asked. "What do you mean by a check?"

"Why, sir, the driver put on the brakes all of a sudden, and I went along the train to see if anything was wrong. And as I passed Sir Wilfred's compartment, I saw him lying back in his corner, just as if he'd gone off to sleep. And he hadn't moved when I saw him again here, poor gentleman."

"You didn't open the door, but just looked through the window?"

"That's right, sir. I thought if I unlocked the door and pushed it back, I might wake him and he wouldn't like it."

"What time was this?"

"We ran through Blackdown Station at 5.29, sir. It would have been three or four minutes later that I passed Sir Wilfred's compartment."

"Did the train actually stop in the tunnel?"

"No, sir, but it slowed down to not more than a few miles an hour. The driver told me that he saw a red light ahead, and put on his brakes. Then, just before he got to it, it changed to green, and he went on. Some chap working on the line, he reckons. But I can't make that out, for there was nothing about it in the notices."

The station-master put in a word of explanation. "Drivers are always warned of the sections where they may expect to find men working on the line," he said.

Arnold nodded. "You say, Turner, that Sir Wilfred had not moved between the time you saw him in the tunnel, and the time you went along to unlock the door. Are you sure of that?"

"Well, sir, he was in exactly the same position the second time as he was the first. He may have moved in between whiles. That I can't say."

"Are you perfectly certain that the door was still locked when you reached here?"

"Perfectly, sir, for I had to use my key to unlock it."

"Was this the only door in the train which was locked?"

"Well, no, sir, not exactly. There was a door at each end of the first-class coach, and these were locked. Passengers have been known to walk along from a third to a first after the train has started. So, unless there is a restaurant car on the train, we always keep the doors in the corridor locked between the firsts and the thirds."

"And these doors were locked from the time the train left Cannon Street until it reached here?"

"That's right, sir. I unlocked them when I went along the train in the tunnel, and locked them again when I went back to my van. They weren't unlocked again till I went through just before we got here."

Arnold had nothing more to ask the guard. He thanked Mr. Cutbush for his assistance, and left the railway station with Marden, carrying the articles found in the compartment. "I'd better have a look at the body, I suppose," he said. "I suppose you've looked through his pockets? No letter, or anything like that?"

"The body is in the mortuary, and so are his clothes and the things found in them. It's only ten minutes walk from here. No, I found no letter. And yet it's a pretty clear case of suicide. What the guard told us seems to settle that. Sir Wilfred was in a locked compartment by himself, all the time."

"Yes," said Arnold, with a faint suspicion of doubt in his tone. "But, do you know, I'm never quite easy in my mind about locked doors, especially when they are railway carriage doors. You know what a simple thing the key of these locks is. Merely a tapered piece of steel, of square cross section. You put it in a square hole, turn it, and the door is unlocked. Anybody could make a key like that. All they would want is a piece of metal rod and a file. Besides, the outer door of the compartment, the one opposite the corridor, I mean, was not locked."

Marden smiled. "You're not suggesting that somebody climbed along the footboard and got in that way, are you?" he asked.

"I'm not suggesting anything. But, before we can dismiss this affair as a case of suicide, we've got to think out all the possibilities. I must say I would like to know more about that slowing down of the train in the tunnel. I am rather struck by a coincidence in time. You tell me that Dr. Frant examined the body about twenty minutes past six yesterday evening, and gave as his opinion that Sir Wilfred had been dead hardly an hour. That's a very vague expression, but I know that doctors can't be exactly accurate in these matters. Let's accept it for what it is worth. According to Turner, the train passed through Blackdown station at 5.29, and entered the tunnel a minute or two later. Doesn't that suggest that Sir Wilfred's death may have taken place in the tunnel, just before Turner saw him?"

"I think it does. But anybody who meant to shoot himself in a train would probably do it in a tunnel. I often go backwards and forwards to London, and I know Blackdown Tunnel pretty well. If the train is going at any speed, there is such a roar that you can't hear yourself shout. Certainly nobody in the next compartment could possibly hear the faint crack those little automatics make."

"There's something in that," Arnold agreed. "And then, of course, there is the fact that he wanted a carriage to himself, and tipped the guard pretty heavily to secure it. By the way, is there any local gossip which might suggest a reason for suicide?"

"None that I know of. Sir Wilfred was very generally respected, and was supposed to be a man of very considerable means. Here we are at the mortuary."

They went in, and Arnold inspected the face of the dead man. He appeared to be between sixty and seventy, clean-shaven, and with thin grey hair. The features were strong and well-chiselled, and even in death there was a firmness of expression which gave the key to Sir Wilfred's character. A man of strong will and intellectual power, Arnold felt sure. Would such a man commit suicide? Not in a fit of sudden depression, certainly. But if a motive existed, which after due and prolonged consideration seemed to him adequate, he would do so without fear or hesitation.

Arnold turned from the body to the clothes, which he examined carefully. There was nothing remarkable about them, being just what a man in Sir Wilfred's position might be expected to wear. On a table beside the clothes lay the contents of the pockets. There were as follows: a bunch of keys, with a silver chain and loop; a small quantity of change, silver and copper; a gold hunter watch with a fine gold chain, and a spectacle case containing a pair of tortoiseshell-rimmed spectacles.

"He was wearing his glasses when he was found," said Marden, as Arnold came to this item. "I found the case in his pocket, and put them into it for safety."

Arnold nodded, and continued his inventory. A gold cigar-case, engraved with the initials W.S., and containing three cigars of an expensive brand. A gold match-box, containing half a dozen Swan vestas. And finally a leather wallet, with gold mounted corners.

Arnold opened this and ran through its contents. These were not numerous. A few visiting cards, with the address of Mavis Court. A book of postage stamps, of which two or three had been torn out. Three five-pound notes, seven one-pound notes, and two ten-shilling notes.

"Well, if he didn't kill himself, the motive for shooting him wasn't robbery," said Arnold. "But there's one thing you missed in turning out his pockets, Mr. Marden."

"What's that?" inquired Marden suspiciously.

"Why, his railway ticket. Unless you've given it up to the company?"

Marden shook his head. "I haven't seen it," he replied.

Arnold searched the pockets for himself. They were empty, and there was no sign of a ticket. "That's queer," he said. "Perhaps in that attaché-case of his. I expect one of these keys will open it."

His guess was correct, and the attaché-case was soon opened. It contained nothing but a few printed papers, reports and statements of accounts, all headed "Wigland and Bunthorne, Ltd., 5 Shrubb Court, London, E.C.3." Glancing at them, Arnold noticed that Sir Wilfred Saxonby, Bart., J.P., was described as the chairman of the firm. Another name caught his eye. Richard K. Saxonby, Esq., Managing Director. "Is that Sir Wilfred's son?" he asked.

"I believe so," Marden replied. "I couldn't be sure."

Arnold put the papers back in the case, and locked it again. "There's no ticket there," he said. "Now, what can he have done with it? It isn't by any chance in his hat, is it?"

Search of the hat, a nearly new bowler, failed to reveal the ticket, and Arnold frowned. "He must have had a ticket," he said. "They wouldn't have let him past the barrier at Cannon Street without one. It's not here, and he can't have dropped it in the compartment, or we should have found it just now. What's become of it?"

Marden shrugged his shoulders. Clearly he thought that this man from Scotland Yard was attaching undue importance to trifles. Sir

Wilfred had shot himself, any fool could see that. What on earth did his ticket matter? He was beyond prosecution for travelling without one. But Marden did not give expression to these thoughts. "He may have dropped it on the platform at Cannon Street," he replied. "It hardly matters, does it?"

"Details like that have a way of mattering," Arnold replied. "However, we can leave the ticket for the moment. I'd like a word with Dr. Frant, before we go out to Mavis Court."

Marden led him to the doctor's house. They found him at home, and quite ready to give information. "Self-inflicted?" he said, in reply to Arnold's question. "Yes, certainly the wound could have been self-inflicted. You found the pistol, did you? H'm. I rather thought you would. A small automatic? Just so, just so. The pistol must have been held horizontally, pointing at the region of the heart, with the muzzle not more than a few inches away. Death, I imagine, was practically instantaneous."

"If Sir Wilfred had held the pistol, would he not have retained it in his grasp after death?" Arnold asked.

"Not necessarily," Dr. Frant replied. "The effect of the bullet entering the heart would very likely be muscular reaction, causing the pistol to be thrown, as it were, from the hand."

"We found the pistol just under the opposite seat of the compartment," said Arnold.

"Very much what might be expected. A very slight twitch of the muscles would be sufficient to project the pistol that distance."

Arnold and Marden took leave of the doctor and went to lunch. The meal over, they took a car and drove to Mavis Court.

III

MAVIS COURT WAS A BEAUTIFUL GEORGIAN HOUSE, SURrounded by an extensive park. Arnold was immediately conscious of an atmosphere of wealth and luxury, which was intensified when they were shown into the drawing-room. And here, in a very few moments, Miss Olivia Saxonby joined them.

Arnold put her down at about forty, and immediately noticed the likeness between her and the dead man. She had the same clear-cut features, the same firmness of mouth and chin. But, whereas these had seemed suitable to Sir Wilfred, the effect in his niece was to make her expression hard and unsympathetic. "Please sit down," she said coldly. "You have come about the death of my uncle, I suppose?"

"I regret that is the purpose of our visit," Arnold replied. "You are Sir Wilfred's niece, I understand. He has a son, has he not?"

"Yes, Dick, who is in America just now. I sent him a cable last night, and have a reply that he is returning immediately."

"Had Sir Wilfred any other children?"

"Yes, a daughter, Irene. She married Major Wardour some years ago; they, too, are abroad, motoring in the south of France. I have wired to their last address, and so far have had no reply."

"Was Sir Wilfred in the habit of going abroad frequently?"

"Not of recent years. He went to Belgium for a week or two last autumn, in connection with his business. Since then he has not spent a night away from here."

"Was he in the habit of going up to London regularly?"

"He went up every Thursday, as a regular thing. Most weeks he went up on some other day as well, usually Tuesday or Wednesday. This week, for instance, he went up on Tuesday."

"Did he always go and return by the same train?"

"He always went up by the 9.50, and nearly always came back by the 6.7. Three or four times a year, however, he would dine in London, and then he came down by the 10.37."

"You have lived with your uncle for some time, Miss Saxonby?"

It seemed to Arnold that her expression hardened as she replied. "Ten years next June. Ever since Aunt Mary died. Uncle Wilfred wanted some member of the family to come and live with him, and, since Dick and Irene were both married, I was the next choice."

"I see. Now, Miss Saxonby, I'm afraid that I shall have to ask some rather distressing questions. During the ten years that you lived with him, you must have got to know Sir Wilfred fairly intimately. You would, I imagine, be the first to detect any change in his health or manner. Did you notice any such change recently?"

Olivia Saxonby shook her head. "I noticed nothing, and Uncle Wilfred was not the sort of person to talk about his health. He seemed just the same, in every way, as I have always known him."

"You know of nothing which might have disturbed his peace of mind in any way?"

"If anything had disturbed him, I should not have known of it. He never spoke to me of business, or, for that matter, of anything important. My business has been to behave like a cheerful companion, and see that the house was properly run."

"You saw Sir Wilfred before he left the house yesterday?"

"Of course. I breakfasted with him at half-past eight, and saw him off in the car when he drove to the station."

"Sir Wilfred had firearms in his possession, had he not?"

"Firearms? Oh, guns and things. Yes, there are some in the gun-room. I'll show them to you."

She took them through the house to the gunroom. There they found a fine collection of sporting guns, also a rifle and a revolver, both of rather antiquated pattern. They also found a quantity of ammunition, but among this were no cartridges to fit the automatic pistol. Arnold had this in his pocket. He produced it, and showed it to Miss Saxonby. "Have you ever seen this before?" he asked.

She merely glanced at it, and shook her head. "My uncle was not in the habit of showing me his guns," she replied.

"You see that it has your uncle's initials on it, Miss Saxonby," Arnold persisted. "Now, it is rather a curious thing that none of these firearms have any initials upon them. Can you suggest why this pistol should have?"

"I can't offer any suggestion. I don't know anything about it. Somebody may have given it to Uncle Wilfred, and had his initials put on it. That's all I can think of."

After some further conversation, in the course of which they ascertained that Sir Wilfred's regular medical attendant was Dr. Butler, of Helverden, Arnold and Marden left Mavis Court.

"I can't help thinking that Miss Saxonby is not overwhelmed with sorrow at her uncle's death," Arnold remarked. "However, that's her business, not ours. She wasn't altogether a mine of information, was she? I think we'd better go and see this doctor chap. He may be able to tell us something."

Dr. Butler proved to be an elderly man of benevolent aspect. He had already heard of the death of Sir Wilfred, and seemed greatly distressed. "He'll be a great loss to the neighbourhood," he said. "He took the lead in every kind of social work, and his name nearly always headed the subscription list. I have heard very few details of his death, but from those I have heard, it seems to me to have been a very extraordinary affair."

"Confidentially, doctor, it looks very much like a case of suicide," Arnold replied. "That's why we've come to see you. Now, I'm not going to ask you to infringe the rules of professional secrecy. But perhaps you can tell me whether or not Sir Wilfred enjoyed good health?"

Dr. Butler considered this question. "He was, in most respects, in perfect health," he replied. "I do not think that there will be any harm in my mentioning the exception, since many people are aware of it already. Sir Wilfred made no particular secret of it. Many years ago, shortly after his wife died, he complained to me of slight indisposition. I diagnosed this as some form of kidney trouble, and sent him up to see a specialist.

"The report was that the kidneys were undoubtedly affected, but that, with proper care, there was no reason to suppose that the fact would endanger the patient's life. He might live to be a hundred. On the other hand, there was just a possibility that complications might ensue at some time, when the matter would become serious. The specialist recommended a diet, to which Sir Wilfred adhered strictly. So far as I am able to judge, his condition had certainly become no worse than when he first consulted me."

"When did you see him last, doctor?" Arnold asked.

"On Monday. I made a habit of looking in on Mondays, as I knew I was pretty certain to find him at home. I asked him if he had had any symptoms of trouble recently, and he told me that he had never felt better in his life. I took samples, which, at the specialist's suggestion, had become a matter of routine, and they showed, if anything, an improvement."

"You knew Sir Wilfred fairly well, doctor. Would you be surprised if it were proved that he had taken his own life?"

"In my profession, one very soon becomes proof against surprise. If you ask me whether I believe that he killed himself as a result of concern for his health, my reply is most emphatically, no! But there are other reasons which might lead a man in his position to such a step."

"Business worries, for instance?"

"Business worries might be among them. Though of recent years Sir Wilfred had not taken a very active part in business. The actual management of the firm is in the hands of his son, Dick."

"Sir Wilfred was, to all appearances, a rich man?"

"A very rich man, I should say. Mavis Court has always been kept up regardless of expense. If any cause of which he approved was in need of funds, he was always ready with a generous cheque. I have no doubt at all that his will will be proved at a very high figure."

"His son and daughter will come into the money, I suppose?"

"I suppose so. But I hope he has remembered Olivia Saxonby. She hasn't had the easiest of lives since she has been with him."

"Miss Saxonby's parents are dead?"

Dr. Butler nodded. "Her mother has been dead a long time, and her father died a couple of years ago. He was the black sheep of the family. Long ago, when she was quite a young girl, there was a discreditable affair in which her father was mixed up, and he had to leave the country rather hastily, Sir Wilfred made his niece a small allowance, and she lived with friends until Lady Saxonby's death. Then her uncle sent for her to Mavis Court."

"She must have lived there in considerable comfort, surely?"

"Comfort? Oh, no doubt. But comfort isn't everything, even to a woman. She was, in a sense, her own mistress before she came to Mavis Court. She could, within the limits of her income, of course, go where she liked, do what she liked, see whom she liked. But at Mavis Court she must have found things very different. Sir Wilfred had peculiar ideas, in some ways. You couldn't call him unsociable, for when you got over his reserve, and could interest him sufficiently, he turned out a very pleasant companion indeed. But he hated having people at Mavis Court. Their presence irritated him, I think because he disliked performing the duties of a host. He always said that his time was too valuable to waste in talking nonsense. And, since his niece did not like to go and see people whom she could not invite back again, she often went from one week's end to another without seeing anybody but her uncle and the staff at Mavis Court."

"She could have left Sir Wilfred, if she found life with him irksome?"

"Oh, yes, she could have left. Her uncle would have ordered the car to take her to the station, I have no doubt. But in his eyes she would have broken her contract. No further allowance would have been forthcoming. And she couldn't possibly afford to risk that."

"Was Sir Wilfred aware that she was discontented?"

"I have never said that she was discontented. I merely remarked that she must have found life at Mavis Court very different from the freedom which she had known previously. Even had she been discontented, and her uncle had been aware of it, it would have made no difference to him whatever. He was one of those people who always knew what was best for other people. Inspector Marden, here, who has heard him on the Bench often enough, will tell you that. Am I right, Marden?"

The inspector smiled. "Quite right, doctor," he replied. "And I seem to remember that business of the Floods Relief Committee."

Dr. Butler made an aggressive grimace. "Yes, that was a very awkward business. We had very serious floods here a few years ago. A lot of damage was done, and some poor people rendered homeless. A fund was got up, and Sir Wilfred became Chairman of the Committee to administer it. But when the wretched sufferers applied for relief, he seemed to consider that unless they ordered their lives in accordance with his ideas, they were not entitled to it, which, not unnaturally, caused a lot of ill-feeling.

"However, we're getting away from the point. I was saying that Sir Wilfred always knew what was best for other people. No doubt he thought that the seclusion of Mavis Court was the best thing for his niece. He had, I fancy, a lurking suspicion that if she were allowed too much rope, she might run off the rails in some way. Hereditary tendency, you know, and that sort of thing. Nobody's affair but her own if she chose to make a fool of herself, of course. I can almost hear Sir Wilfred say so. But he wasn't going to risk a second family scandal, for all that."

All this, though it had no direct bearing on Sir Wilfred's death, Arnold found very interesting. With a view to encouraging Dr. Butler's confidences he asked provocatively, "Sir Wilfred seems to have been a man who was not afraid of making enemies?"

"Afraid?" the doctor replied. "I don't believe he was afraid of anything, morally or physically. But I'm not so sure about making enemies. We none of us know how we arouse hostility in other people, unless we definitely set out to do so. And that Sir Wilfred never did. For one thing, he had a very strong sense of justice, and, for another, he had no time to waste in quarrelling with people. He was disliked by many people who didn't know him properly, and who took offence at his rather overbearing manner. But I don't believe that he had a really active enemy in the world."

"You haven't heard any rumours affecting his financial position, have you, doctor?" Arnold asked.

Dr. Butler shook his head. "Finance and business are a bit outside my scope," he replied. "I've heard no rumours of the kind, but then it's not likely that they would come to my ears. I gather that you are looking for something to support the idea that he committed suicide?"

"That's about it, doctor. And I should be very grateful for the slightest hint."

"I can't help you, I'm afraid. You can take it from me that there's no disreputable story behind it. No entanglements with women, or anything like that. For the rest, Sir Wilfred was a man of temperate, not to say frugal habits. You can trust a doctor to know something about his patients' lives. I can tell you nothing about his business activities. But of this I feel sure. If he had a motive for killing himself, you won't find that motive in Helverden."

A few minutes later, Arnold and Marden left the doctor's house and drove back to Stourford, where Arnold met the local superintendent. "I hardly know what to say, yet," he replied, in answer to the latter's inquiries. "Everything seems to point to suicide, but so far I haven't been able to get any hint as to the motive. You knew him pretty well yourself, sir?"

"Yes, I've known him for a good many years, and always managed to get on with him. Between ourselves, he was a man I respected rather than liked. He wasn't altogether the sort of character who inspires affection. And I can assure you that he would never have killed himself unless he had some very excellent reason for doing so. In the case of a man like Sir Wilfred, you and I needn't believe in what is charitably known as temporary insanity."

Arnold nodded. "There's one point I should like your opinion upon, sir. You know that Mr. Marden found in the compartment an automatic with the initials W.S. upon it. It seems to me rather queer that a magistrate, the chairman of the Bench, in fact, should commit the offence of having a pistol in his possession without taking out a certificate for it. Especially as I understand that he has a certificate for two other weapons."

"That's a good point," replied the superintendent approvingly. "I'll give you my opinion willingly. Sir Wilfred was an excellent and conscientious magistrate, and I don't think he made many mistakes while he was on the Bench. But he always gave me the impression that he considered himself as beyond the law. The law was an excellent thing, and he was a firm supporter of it. But it was made for other people, rather than for Sir Wilfred Saxonby.

"I don't mean that he habitually broke the law, or even that I know of a single instance in which he did so. But I feel pretty certain that he would have had no scruple about breaking the law, if it suited his own higher convenience. He would not have felt himself bound by restrictions which, in other cases, he would have been the first to enforce.

"This being so, you will understand my opinion. If Sir Wilfred had acquired a pistol for any ordinary purpose, he would not have hesitated to take out a certificate for it. On the other hand, if he acquired it for some purpose to which it was essential that it should not be suspected that he had it, the omission to take out a certificate would not have troubled his conscience. Is that clear?"

"Perfectly clear, sir," Arnold replied. He felt that he had now some idea of the dead man's character. Two things remained to be done. To discover a motive which might have induced Sir Wilfred to take his own life, and to eliminate any possibility of the shot having been fired by some other hand. He parted from the superintendent and Marden, and returned to the railway station.

IV

ARRIVED AT THE STATION, ARNOLD SOUGHT MR. CUTBUSH IN his office, to which, at his request, the booking clerk was summoned. The latter remembered perfectly selling Sir Wilfred a ticket on the previous morning. It had been a first-class day return to London. The return half of this ticket had not been handed in.

Having secured this information, Arnold took the next train, which happened to be a fast one, to Blackdown. During the journey, he pondered the question of the missing ticket. It was a trifling circumstance, as Marden had remarked. Anything might have happened. It might have fallen out of Sir Wilfred's pocket while his body was being carried from the compartment to the waiting-room, for instance. But supposing it hadn't? Suppose it had passed from Sir Wilfred's possession between the times of his passing the barrier at Cannon Street and his arrival at Stourford. What then?

Arnold repeated the question to himself without finding any plausible answer. It was ridiculous to suggest that it had been stolen from Sir Wilfred, either before or after his death. Who would steal a railway ticket, and leave behind valuables and a sum of money? Besides, how could anybody have obtained access to the locked compartment? Easily enough, if they had a railway key. But could they have done so without attracting notice? It seemed highly improbable. Arnold decided that it would be necessary to interrogate the other twenty-four passengers who had travelled in the first-class coach.

His train arrived at the entrance to Blackdown Tunnel as he reached this decision. Before it had travelled many yards farther, the windows of his compartment were rendered opaque by a mixture of smoke and steam deposited on the outside. And the roar was certainly loud enough to drown the report of a small pistol. Arnold noted these things. He also timed the passage of the train through the tunnel. It took three minutes and twenty-five seconds. Allowing for the slowing up and acceleration, the train in which Sir Wilfred had been travelling must have taken at least five minutes. And a lot can happen in five minutes, as Arnold knew well enough.

Shortly after emerging from the tunnel, the train pulled up at Blackdown station. Arnold got out, and sought the station-master, to whom he introduced himself. He explained that he was investigating the death of Sir Wilfred Saxonby, who had been found dead the previous day on the arrival at Stourford of the five o'clock train from Cannon Street. "And there's some reason to believe that he died in Blackdown Tunnel," he added.

"In the tunnel, eh?" the station-master replied. "That's not the only queer thing that happened in the tunnel yesterday evening. The driver of that very train reported that he was held up in the tunnel by a man waving a red light. He must have dreamt it, for there was certainly nobody there."

"Can you be sure of that?" Arnold asked.

"As sure as that I'm talking to you now. I'll explain why. To begin with, the tunnel isn't exactly the place one would choose for an evening stroll. The public don't use it as a promenade, so to speak. The only people who ever go into it on foot are the permanent way men. And, during the whole of yesterday, none of these men set foot inside it. Besides, they don't go in singly. They go in a gang, and light flares. The driver reports no flares, only a red light which changed to green just before he reached it.

"Now, I know what you're going to say. If it wasn't one of the permanent way men, it must have been some unauthorised person who had somehow wandered in. Well, I say it couldn't have been, and for this reason. At each end of the tunnel there is a signal cabin, and nobody could possibly get in without being seen by the men on duty. Even after dark a strong light shines from the windows of the cabins on to the line. There's no question of a man slipping past in a fog, for it was perfectly clear yesterday evening. I've questioned the men on duty at both ends, and they swear that nobody can have gone in or out.

"But I wasn't satisfied with that. It struck me that perhaps, by some miracle, somebody might have got into the tunnel and been run over. So, as soon as I heard about the driver's report, I sent a search party through, to look for a body, or bits of one. Of course, they found nothing of the kind. I never for a moment expected that they would. You may take it from me, inspector, that there was nobody in the tunnel yesterday evening."

"Then how do you account for the driver's report?" Arnold asked.

The station-master shrugged his shoulders.

"Tunnels are queer places," he replied. "You've never been through one, except in a train, I suppose? And then you're nice and comfortable, and you run through so quick that you don't have time to notice things. If you'd ever been through on foot, you wouldn't want to repeat the experience. It's pitch dark, to begin with, and then it's usually full of smoke and steam, unless the wind happens to be blowing through it.

"I can imagine a driver, even an experienced man, imagining that he saw a light. Maybe a reflection in the window of his cab, or something like that. He'd naturally pull up, for we believe in safety first on the railway, whatever they may think on the roads. And when he saw that it wasn't a red light at all, but only a reflection, he'd go ahead again.

"But he'd have to account for slowing down. And he wouldn't care to make himself look a fool by saying that he thought he saw a red light when there hadn't been one there at all. So he'd make up a yarn like this, about the red light that turned to green, and his fireman would back him up. And that, you'll find, is about the truth of it."

After this conversation with the station-master at Blackdown, Arnold continued his journey to London. The engine-driver's report seemed to be disposed of. The train had certainly slowed down in the tunnel, that at least was an established fact. But only because of an hallucination on the part of the driver. He had seen a red and a green light where none could have existed. Rather an uncanny happening, if those lights had been seen at the moment of Sir Wilfred's death. Could the flash of the pistol have had anything to do with it? By some extraordinary trick of reflection, could the driver have seen this flash as a red light ahead of him? Not under ordinary circumstances, Arnold imagined. But, as the station-master had said, tunnels were queer places.

He arrived at Cannon Street, and there made a few further inquiries. As a result of these he learnt that passengers had to show their tickets at the barrier before obtaining access to the platforms. The ticket inspector who had been on duty the previous evening happened to know Sir Wilfred by sight. He remembered punching his ticket, the return half of a first-class to Stourford. At the barrier, Sir Wilfred had extracted the ticket from a leather wallet, from which at the same time he took a pound note. The ticket inspector believed that, after his ticket had been examined, Sir Wilfred had put it back in the wallet. When he reached the platform, he stopped and spoke to the guard, and they had walked up the train together. Sir Wilfred had been carrying an attaché-case, but no other luggage.

This confirmed Turner's statement, but threw no fresh light on the mystery of the ticket. In fact, it rather tended to deepen that mystery. If Sir Wilfred had put it back in his wallet, the possibility of it having fallen out at Stourford was removed. Arnold made a mental note of this, as one of the puzzling but possibly irrelevant features of the case. He then walked to Shrubb Court, and entered the imposing offices of Messrs Wigland and Bunthorne.

The death of the chairman of the company did not seem to have upset the decorous routine of the place. Arnold handed in his card, and asked to see the secretary. He was received by a pleasant, energetic-looking man of about forty, tall, clean-shaven and muscular, who introduced himself as Mr. Torrance. "You've come about this most unfortunate affair of Sir Wilfred, I suppose, inspector?" he said. "Make yourself comfortable, and I'll try to answer your questions as well as I can."

"That's very good of you, Mr. Torrance," Arnold replied. "In the first place, I'd be glad to know something of the firm of Wigland and Bunthorne, and the position which Sir Wilfred held in it."

"That's an easy one to start with, inspector. We are importers of produce, mainly from the East. Tea, coffee, rubber, spices, almost everything you can think of. The business was started in a small way over a hundred years ago by two partners, the original Wigland and Bunthorne. Their successors were bought out some fifty years ago by Oscar Saxonby, Sir Wilfred's father. Oscar became Lord Mayor, and received a baronetcy. At his death, Sir Wilfred succeeded him. When his son, Richard, came of age, he made the business into a private company, with himself as chairman, and Richard and two others as directors. For some time after that Sir Wilfred took an active part in the management. But, shortly after Lady Saxonby's death, Richard Saxonby was appointed managing director, and his father practically handed over the direction of the business to him. Since then Sir Wilfred has confined himself to attending directors' meetings, and coming up here once, and occasionally twice a week."

"What did he do on those occasions?"

"Either one of the directors or myself would give him a sort of résumé of the past week. He would comment upon this, and make suggestions. Then he would study the various market reports. He had a room of his own here, where he could sit without being disturbed. I will show it to you, if you care to see it."

"I should like to do so later. Sir Wilfred was here yesterday, I understand?"

"He was. I did not see him personally, as I had gone to Manchester, where we have a branch office. However, my assistant was with him shortly before he left here to catch his train home."

"You had, however, seen him fairly recently, I suppose, Mr. Torrance?"

"I saw him on the previous Thursday, the seventh, and spent a considerable time with him in his room."

"Then you may be able to tell me whether you noticed any change in Sir Wilfred lately. Did he seem the same, when you last saw him, as you had always known him?"

Torrance hesitated. "Well, to all appearances he seemed the same. But I happen to know that he had something on his mind, for he discussed it with me that very day."

"I don't want to ask indiscreet questions, Mr. Torrance," said Arnold. "But was this something connected with the business?"

"Oh, dear no, nothing like that. I may as well tell you at once that Sir Wilfred had no business worries. He didn't trouble himself about the minor matters which are the principal sources of anxiety to heads of departments. And, for the rest, the firm's affairs are in an exceptionally flourishing condition. We escaped the worst consequences of the depression, and since the recent improvement in trade we have gone ahead rapidly. Sir Wilfred, when I saw him, was very pleased with a report from Mr. Richard—Sir Richard, as he is now—who is in America. He said himself that the prospects of the firm were never brighter."

"Then he felt no concern over his financial affairs?"

"Not the slightest. He had no occasion to do so. But he was worried, in my opinion rather unduly worried, about his daughter, Mrs. Wardour. She and Major Wardour have not been hitting it off for some time past. How serious their disagreement is, I do not know, though Mrs. Wardour, who is now one of our directors, has made disparaging remarks about her husband in my hearing. But Sir Wilfred must have taken a particularly gloomy view, for he asked me about the legal aspect of separation. And I could see that he was very much worried over the situation that had arisen."

"Major and Mrs. Wardour are now motoring in the South of France, are they not?"

"Yes, at Sir Wilfred's suggestion. I think he had an idea that if they went together away from their usual surroundings, they might find a means of composing their differences. I may say that there was a letter from Mrs. Wardour awaiting him here yesterday."

"Was it usual for Mrs. Wardour to write to her father here, and not at Mavis Court?"

"Not unusual. Sir Wilfred used to have a good deal of his correspondence addressed here. Mainly, I think, because there was a typist available, and he could dictate the replies. Any letters that came for him were laid on his table, to await his next visit. Naturally I know Mrs. Wardour's handwriting, and I noticed this letter. It bore a French stamp, and arrived here on Tuesday. I put it on Sir Wilfred's table myself that morning."

A rather curious idea passed through Arnold's mind. "Richard Saxonby's visit to America is connected with the affairs of the firm, I understand. Was it undertaken at Sir Wilfred's suggestion?"

"Yes, decidedly. We have considerable interests there, and for some time Sir Wilfred had maintained that one of the directors should go over and observe conditions at first hand. At one time he spoke of going himself, but he abandoned the idea not long ago, and urged Mr. Richard to go instead. He said that the trip would do him good, and that if he took his wife they would both enjoy it."

"And Richard Saxonby fell in with his father's suggestion?"

"People usually fell in with Sir Wilfred's suggestions," replied Torrance dryly.

Arnold nodded. He had gathered as much already. "Do you think I might see your assistant, whom you mentioned as having seen Sir Wilfred yesterday?" he asked.

The assistant secretary was sent for. He was an older man than Torrance, and Arnold guessed that he had risen from the position of chief clerk. He had been in attendance on Sir Wilfred all day, off and on. Sir Wilfred had arrived at the office between half-past eleven and twelve. There were perhaps a dozen letters awaiting him. One of these he had picked up, read, and laid aside.

He had then asked for the usual résumé, which he had read and discussed with various members of the firm. This had occupied him until shortly after one, when he had gone out to lunch. He came back about two, and shortly afterwards sent for a typist, to whom he dictated half a dozen letters. Some further papers, dealing with matters of routine, and of no particular importance, were put before him. In the course of the afternoon he had a visitor, a well-dressed young man, who gave the name of Yates, and said he had an appointment with Sir Wilfred. On being informed of his visit, Sir Wilfred gave orders that he was to be shown up to his room at once. He remained there for ten minutes, certainly not longer, then went away. He and Sir Wilfred were alone in the latter's room during the interview.

Neither Torrance nor his assistant were acquainted with this man Yates. The latter was of the opinion that he had called upon a personal matter, since Sir Wilfred had made no subsequent allusion to his visitor.

Asked if he had noticed anything unusual in Sir Wilfred's manner during the day, the assistant secretary replied that he had not. He had seemed much the same as usual, except for one trifling incident. At about a quarter to five he had ordered a taxi to be sent for, and had told the man to drive him to Cannon Street Station.

"A taxi!" exclaimed Torrance, who obviously heard this for the first time. "I never knew him do that before. He wasn't ill, or anything? You're sure of that?"

"There didn't seem to me to be anything the matter with him," replied the assistant secretary. "And I've known him, man and boy, for the last forty years and more."

"That's peculiar," said Torrance. "As you know, inspector, it's only a few hundred yards from here to Cannon Street. Sir Wilfred always walked it, whatever the weather was like. I've never known him take a taxi before. It's most unlike him. And now, perhaps, you'd like to come and see his room?"

Arnold agreed, and they went along the passage to a door which Torrance opened with a key. "It's always kept locked," he explained. "Sir Wilfred had one key, Mr. Richard another, and I have the third. The only person who has been in here since Sir Wilfred left yesterday afternoon is myself. I came in this morning to see if he had left any message for me. But, finding there was none, I touched nothing, and came out at once. That was before I heard of Sir Wilfred's death."

"How did the news reach you, Mr. Torrance?" Arnold asked.

"Miss Olivia Saxonby telephoned to the office about ten o'clock this morning. She said that her uncle had been found shot in the train. Of course, I asked her for particulars, but she said that she knew no more, but from what she had heard she gathered that he had committed suicide."

Arnold made no comment upon this, but he wondered what grounds Miss Olivia could have had for her opinion, as early as ten o'clock that morning. Then he remembered that Sir Wilfred's car had been waiting for him at Stourford Station. No doubt the chauffeur had gleaned such scraps of information as were available, and had carried them to Mavis Court.

He turned his attention to the room, thickly carpeted and luxuriously furnished. The most conspicuous feature was a heavy mahogany table, upon which stood a couple of letter trays, holding a few sheets of correspondence. Beside the table was a waste-paper basket, holding a few fragments of torn letters.

"I wonder if you would mind looking for the letter from Mrs. Wardour, Mr. Torrance?" said Arnold.

Torrance ran through the trays, then turned his attention to the waste-paper basket. "I can't see any signs of it, or of the envelope, for that matter," he reported at last. "I dare say Sir Wilfred put it in his pocket and took it home with him. The rest of this stuff is of no importance, but perhaps you'd like to look through it?"

Arnold did so, without discovering anything that could throw light upon Sir Wilfred's death. Half a dozen letters upon indifferent subjects, as many appeals for subscriptions to various charities. Nor were the carbon copies of the letters dictated by Sir Wilfred on the previous day any more informative.

There was a large filing-cabinet in the room, and Arnold pointed to this. "What's in there?" he asked.

Torrance shook his head. "I don't know," he replied. "It's locked, and Sir Wilfred is the only person who had a key to it. I have an idea that he used to put his personal letters in it."

The front of the cabinet was closed by a sliding shutter, fitted with a lock. In order to demonstrate his words, Torrance went up to it, and tried to raise the shutter. "Well, I'm damned!" he exclaimed. "It isn't locked, after all! That's the most extraordinary thing. There certainly must have been something on Sir Wilfred's mind yesterday. I've never before known him to leave this cabinet unlocked."

"Well, we may as well see what's inside it," said Arnold. Their search revealed nothing but a mass of correspondence, all carefully filed. As in the case of the other letters, there was nothing in there which could be considered in any way out of the ordinary. But, as Arnold drew out one of the documents, he heard something rattling. He removed the files it contained, and beneath them found half a dozen small metal objects. They were pistol cartridges, exactly similar in appearance to those which had been found in the magazine of the automatic.

Arnold picked them out of the drawer, and laid them on the table. "Can you account for these, Mr. Torrance?" he asked.

Torrance shook his head. "No, I can't," he replied. "They have probably been there a long time. Years ago, when I first knew him, Sir Wilfred was very fond of target shooting, and was a very good shot, both with rifle and revolver. But recently, I believe, he had given it up. I expect these are the remains of some cartridges which he used to keep here."

Arnold made no comment upon this. He put the cartridges in his pocket, and helped Torrance to replace the correspondence in the drawer. "By the way," he remarked, while they were thus engaged, "has your firm got any connections in Belgium?"

"Belgium?" Torrance replied. "We've got connections all over the world, and in Belgium, among other countries."

"I am told that Sir Wilfred paid a visit to Belgium last summer. Was this on a matter of business?"

"Not to my knowledge. Sir Wilfred liked spending a few days abroad, from time to time. He may have called upon one or two people in Brussels and Antwerp with whom we do business, but only in a friendly way."

"When do you expect Richard Saxonby?"

"We had a cable from him to-day, saying that he would arrive at Southampton on the 23rd. I presume that Miss Olivia had informed him of Sir Wilfred's death."

Arnold had no further inquiries to make, and he returned to Scotland Yard.

V

DESMOND MERRION HAPPENED TO BE STAYING FOR A FEW DAYS in London, at his rooms in St. James's. He was something of an amateur criminologist, and a friend of Arnold's. So, when he received a telephone call from the Inspector, suggesting that they should dine together that Friday evening, he guessed that Arnold was engaged upon some case which presented points of interest.

But he was rather surprised when he heard that Arnold had been engaged upon investigating the death of Sir Wilfred Saxonby. "I've read what the papers have to say," he said. "And, to all appearances, it seemed a pretty obvious case of suicide. I'm astonished that the Yard should have been called in at all. The importance of Sir Wilfred's position accounts for it, I suppose?"

"That's about it," Arnold replied. "I don't think there's much room for doubt that Sir Wilfred shot himself. But the papers don't know quite as much as I do. I'd like to tell you what I've heard, and see what you make of it."

He described his investigations in detail. "Now, it strikes me that Sir Wilfred planned his suicide some time in advance," he continued. "He decided that he would shoot himself. He already possessed a revolver, but that was too cumbrous and noisy a weapon for his purpose. A small automatic would be just as deadly, and much more convenient.

"But how was he to get hold of one? As you know, automatic pistols cannot be bought in this country without the production of a firearms certificate. Certainly a man in Sir Wilfred's position would not have had the slightest difficulty in obtaining such a certificate.

But secrecy is a characteristic of the intending suicide. Sir Wilfred would imagine that people would wonder what he wanted an automatic for, and would be afraid that they would guess correctly. It would suit him far better to get hold of one without the necessity of applying for a certificate.

"This would be the simplest thing in the world. He had only to go abroad, buy a pistol while there, and smuggle it in. He was probably known to the customs officers at the port where he landed, and they would not make any very extensive search of his baggage. Besides, a little pistol like that could easily be concealed about the person, and with it a dozen rounds of ammunition."

"You haven't yet traced the purchase of the pistol, have you?" Merrion asked.

"No, but with the help of a firearms expert, I hope to."

"You're probably on the right track. I have only one comment to make. I can't imagine, somehow, that Saxonby bought the pistol for the sole purpose of killing himself with it. Why should he have his initials engraved upon it, if so?"

"I've got an idea about that. I told you, I think, that none of the other firearms at Mavis Court have initials on them. I believe that Sir Wilfred had them engraved upon the automatic for a definite purpose. He wanted it to be quite clear that the pistol was his, to prevent suspicion falling upon anybody else. Suicides do that kind of thing, you know."

"Such as leaving letters behind them, explaining their actions. All right, go ahead."

"Having provided himself with the weapon, Sir Wilfred's next move was to get his family out of the way. I imagine that he hated the idea of any fuss or bother. He would like to be buried and out of the way before his sorrowing relatives could make a scene. At all events, he suggested that his son and his wife should go to America, and his daughter and her husband to the South of France. That, I think, is an indication of what was in his mind."

"Very possibly," Merrion replied. "So far as you know, he took no steps to get his niece out of the way?"

"Apparently not. But perhaps he knew that she would not come into the category of a sorrowing relative. From what I saw and heard, I don't think that Miss Olivia is likely to break her heart over her uncle's death. Sir Wilfred's next step was to decide upon the time and place of his suicide. His dislike of fuss would prevent him from shooting himself either at his office or at Mavis Court. Too many people about. They would rush in at the sound of the shot, and possibly disturb his last moments. He knew the line between London and Stourford well enough, and must have noticed how suitable Blackdown Tunnel was to his purpose. If he could get a carriage to himself, he could fire the shot as the train was passing through the tunnel, and it would be very unlikely that his death would be discovered until it reached Stourford."

"And that, you think, is what actually happened?"

"I'm willing to bet that it is what the coroner and his jury will think. After all, if you find a man dead in a locked railway carriage, with the weapon which killed him within a couple of feet or so, the suggestion of suicide is bound to be pretty strong.

"But, all the same, there are certain objections to the suicide theory. In the first place, I haven't been able to light upon a vestige of reasonable motive. The only hint, so far, is that Sir Wilfred was worried by the disagreement between his daughter and her husband. But I refuse to believe that any amount of friction, however serious, between a daughter and a son-in-law would drive a man to suicide. Certainly not a man like Sir Wilfred. And, after all, the Wardours can't have been on such desperately bad terms, since, apparently, they agreed to go off on a motor tour together."

"I wouldn't jump too hastily to the conclusion that there was a complete lack of motive," said Merrion. "Saxonby was a man of many interests, and you may find that something had gone very seriously wrong somewhere. He may have had something on his mind which he shared with nobody else. What are your other objections to the suicide theory?"

"They are so trifling that they are hardly worth discussing. I'll try to put them as simply as I can. Torrance says that there was a letter from Mrs. Wardour waiting for Sir Wilfred when he reached the office yesterday. The assistant secretary says that when he arrived, he selected one of his letters, read it, and laid it aside. I think we may assume that it was the one from his daughter, since he was anxious about her. Now, where is that letter? It was not to be found in his room, and there is no fire there in which he could have burnt it. Torrance suggests that he put it in his pocket. Most likely he did. But why wasn't it in his pocket when the train reached Stourford? Again, we know that he presented his ticket at the barrier at Cannon Street, and we believe that, having done so, he put it back in his wallet. What became of that ticket?

"There are, of course, a thousand possible explanations of the disappearance of the letter and the ticket. For instance, Sir Wilfred may have thrown them out of the carriage window before the train reached Blackdown. But I can't forget that curious and unexplained incident in the tunnel. Whether the driver actually saw those red and green lights, or whether he only imagined them, the fact remains that the train slowed down to about ten miles an hour or less. You can laugh at me, if you like."

"I'm not likely to do that," Merrion replied. "But I'd like you to explain the possible significance of that slowing down."

"It's hopelessly far-fetched. To begin with, the compartment had two doors. One, the left-hand one, looking towards the engine, led into the corridor, and was locked. The other, the right-hand one, led into the open, and was unlocked. Now, in this country, trains follow the rule of the road, and keep to the left. If anybody was in the tunnel as the train passed through, he would be standing on the up line, to avoid being run over by the train, which was on the down line. It would not have been impossible for him to have jumped upon the footboard, and entered Sir Wilfred's compartment by the unlocked door."

Merrion nodded. "I admit the possibility. We can go further, and say that it would be possible for this man to have shot Saxonby, stolen his ticket and the letter from his daughter, and jumped off the train again. But, apart from the possibility, we are bound to examine the probability of this having happened. And I'm bound to confess that I see a whole host of difficulties in the way. I'll put them to you as they appear to me.

"To begin with, we have the extreme unlikelihood of there having been a man in the tunnel. According to the station-master at Blackdown, that unlikelihood amounts to impossibility. I wouldn't go so far as to accept his statement without further investigation. But, all the same, since he knows more about the conditions than we do, we are bound to attach a certain weight to what he says."

"It has occurred to me that there are other ways of getting into the tunnel than by entering it on foot," said Arnold. "One might jump off a train while it was going through."

"Yes," Merrion replied doubtfully. "I shouldn't care to do it myself, but I suppose it could be done. But I don't suppose many trains slow up as conveniently as the one in which Saxonby was travelling. However, let's admit the bare possibility of there having been a man in the tunnel, who deliberately slowed down the train so that he would be able to board it.

"Now, we pass on to the next point. In order that he could effect his purpose, it would be necessary that Saxonby should be travelling in a compartment by himself, and that his assailant should know which compartment this was. How could he have obtained the knowledge on either of these points? He might, it is true, have guessed that, for some reason with which he was acquainted, Saxonby would want to secure a compartment to himself. But how can he have known that Saxonby had been successful? Or, if he gambled on the probability of this success, how did he know which compartment it was? He couldn't have seen Saxonby through the window, for that would almost certainly be obscured by the fumes from the engine."

"Yes, I'm with you there," said Arnold. "I noticed that for myself, as I was coming through this morning."

"Good. Now we come to the man's procedure. He provides himself with a pistol upon which he has engraved Saxonby's initials. There's nothing unreasonable about that. But, all the same, if the pistol wasn't really Saxonby's, it is peculiar that you should have found ammunition to fit it in his private filing cabinet.

"We needn't, at present, enter into the question of motive. We don't know enough about Saxonby and his affairs. We may find that he had a reasonable and sufficient motive for committing suicide. It is equally possible that we find that somebody had a reasonable and sufficient motive for killing him.

"Finally, there is the disappearance of the ticket and the letter. Now, I'm bound to admit that the theory of a man boarding the train from the tunnel might be twisted to account for that.

"Suppose this man, having shot Saxonby, did not leave the train again immediately. Suppose he unlocked the door leading into the corridor, passed through it, and locked it behind him. Suppose then that he hid in the lavatory until the train reached Stourford, and then got out? But he would need a ticket before he could leave the station. Foreseeing this necessity, he provided himself with Saxonby's ticket."

"That's ingenious!" Arnold exclaimed. "I've always admired your imagination, as you know. And I've got a list of all the passengers who were travelling in that first-class coach."

"You'll probably find that very useful. This imaginary man of ours, having taken the ticket, may also have taken the letter, perhaps because its discovery might have given a clue to his own identity.

"But, in spite of what you choose to call the ingenuity of my arguments, I don't like the theory of the man in the tunnel. It seems to me that the difficulties altogether outweigh the suggestion offered by the ticket. Quite frankly, I don't believe that Saxonby was murdered. I believe that he shot himself. But, if you want a theory of how he might have been murdered, I think I can supply you with one which presents fewer difficulties than that of the man boarding the train in the tunnel."

The Inspector smiled. "I'd love to hear it," he said.

"Then so you shall. It is this. The murderer did not board the train in the tunnel. He left it there. That gets round the worst of the difficulties. Our man knew that Saxonby would be going home by the five o'clock from Cannon Street yesterday. No difficulty about that, for he did so nearly every Thursday. He may have been watching the train every Thursday for weeks, awaiting his opportunity. Yesterday he saw Saxonby installed in a carriage by himself, and realised that his opportunity had come.

"He had provided himself with a first-class ticket, and took a seat in another compartment of the coach. As soon as the train entered the tunnel, he went along the corridor, opened the door of Saxonby's carriage, shot him, relocked the corridor door, and slipped out on to the line through the other door, the train having conveniently slowed down to allow him to do so."

"Well, that's an alternative, certainly," said Arnold thoughtfully. "It disposes of some of the difficulties, but it raises others. If the man was in the train, and not standing on the line in the tunnel, he can't have waved that red light at the driver. How, then, did he know that the train would slow down? What would he have done if it hadn't?"

"Oh, I'm not defending my theory. I only put it forward as a piece of speculative reasoning. But why shouldn't he have a confederate in the tunnel, who worked the lights to slow down the train?"

"No!" exclaimed Arnold decidedly. "That won't do. In spite of the station-master at Blackdown, I'm prepared to believe in the possibility of one man having slipped in or out of the tunnel unobserved. But you ask me to believe that one man got in, and two came out, and that's going too far."

Merrion laughed. "My dear fellow, I quite agree with you," he replied. "I told you that I wasn't defending my theory. But doesn't all this show the difficulty of forming any plausible theory to account for Saxonby having been murdered?"

"I've felt that all along. But I'm bound to think of every possibility, no matter how remote."

"Of course you are. Well, let's see what possibilities there are. We'll assume that Saxonby was shot while the train was passing through the tunnel. He, or any one else, would naturally choose that time, since the report of the pistol would then be effectively drowned. But I don't think we need assume that the slowing down of the train had any connection with the event. It may have been merely a coincidence, due to hallucination on the part of the driver.

"Cutting that out, then, two possibilities remain. The first is that Saxonby was murdered by Turner, the guard. He had plenty of opportunity, but no apparent motive. The second is, that the murderer was some other passenger in the coach, who returned quietly to his own compartment when the deed was done. And, in that case, you ought to be able to identify him. It seems that the only compartment with a single occupant was Saxonby's. By questioning the twenty-four passengers whose names you have, you will be able to find out if anybody left his seat before the train reached the tunnel, and returned to it afterwards."

"I'm going to do that in any case, just as a precaution," Arnold replied.

"Good. And, while you're on the subject of precautions, I wouldn't dismiss the tunnel altogether. I would see the driver and fireman of the train, and try to find out whether they really saw those lights or not. If they admit that they were mistaken, well and good. If not, I would search the tunnel myself."

"Didn't I tell you that it has been searched already?"

Merrion shook his head. "Not really searched," he said. "A party of men went through it, looking for a definite and easily noticeable object, a body. They wouldn't have been on the look-out for anything less conspicuous, such as a first-class railway ticket, for instance. And if they had, they would not have attached any particular importance to it. And, while you were about it, I should have a look at those signal boxes, and satisfy myself that they really do command the approaches to the tunnel as thoroughly as the station-master makes out. I'd always rather see a thing for myself than rely on somebody else's description of it."

Arnold seemed impressed. "I dare say you're right," he replied. "But if the tunnel is to be searched, it ought to be done as soon as possible. If I decide to do it, will you come with me?"

"And imperil my life in the cause of justice? All right, I don't mind."

"Then I'd better get back to the Yard and see about it," said Arnold.

VI

IN THE COURSE OF THE FOLLOWING MORNING, MERRION WAS again rung up by the Inspector. "I've arranged with the company to see those railwaymen," he said. "They're to meet me at Blackdown at two o'clock. If you like, we'll have a spot of lunch somewhere, and catch a train at Charing Cross about one o'clock."

Merrion agreed to this readily enough. In spite of the overwhelming evidence in favour of it, he was bound to admit the possibility of a doubt that Sir Wilfred Saxonby had shot himself. As he had told Arnold, his own belief was that it had been a case of suicide. But belief was not proof, and until all doubt had been removed, suicide could not be accepted as a fact.

He met Arnold as arranged, and they travelled down to Blackdown together. The station-master, who had been instructed by the railway company to hold himself at Arnold's disposition, met them. "The driver and fireman have just arrived," he said. "They are waiting in my office. Will you see them now?"

"Yes, I'll see them," Arnold replied. "But one at a time, I think. I'll begin with the driver. What's his name?"

"Robert Prentice. He has been a driver for fifteen years, and is considered a very steady and reliable man. The fireman's name is Charles Haynes, another very steady chap."

Arnold and Merrion installed themselves in the station-master's room, into which the driver was introduced. "Sit down, Prentice," said Arnold. "I want to ask you a few questions. You were the driver of the five o'clock from Cannon Street on Thursday?"

"That's right, sir. I've been driving that train all the week."

"And you slowed up the train in Blackdown Tunnel?"

The driver's face hardened. "I've already reported why, sir," he replied.

"Yes, I know, and you've been disbelieved. Now, I'm going to be perfectly frank with you, and I'm sure you'll be the same with me. As no doubt you've seen in the papers, a passenger was found shot in the train when it arrived at Stourford. Well, there's reason to believe that the shot was fired in Blackdown Tunnel."

"I saw about the accident, sir," said Prentice. "But I didn't know it happened in the tunnel."

"We believe it did. Now you'll understand why I wanted to talk to you. You reported having seen red and green lights in the tunnel. If you did, the person who showed, those lights may have had something to do with the death of the passenger. But are you quite sure you saw them? If you aren't quite sure, say so, and nobody will blame you in the least."

"I wasn't mistaken," replied Prentice quietly. "I've been through the tunnel too often to imagine lights that aren't there. I saw a red light that changed to green, and I'll take my oath upon that."

"Tell us exactly what you did see," said Arnold.

"I entered the tunnel steaming hard, doing perhaps fifty miles an hour or a bit more. The signals were clear, and there are no more until you get beyond the tunnel on the other side. Often enough, if there's been an up train through just before, the tunnel is so full of smoke and steam that you can't see a flare till you're right on top of it. But on Thursday evening it wasn't so bad, quite clear in the tunnel, you might say, and there was nothing in the notices about men working in it. So I let her rip, giving a long whistle on entering the tunnel, according to regulations.

"I hadn't gone far, in fact I'd just taken my hand off the whistle, when I thought I saw a red light ahead of me. I shut off steam at once, although I didn't see how it could be a light. I thought it must be another train coming towards me, steaming hard, and that the blast had driven a red coal through the funnel. But there the light was, and it seemed to be moving. So I clapped on the brake, and called to my mate to look. He saw the light as plain as I did, and we both knew that something was up.

"Well, sir, you can't pull up a heavy train like you can a motor-car, and I thought we were for it. I couldn't judge how far off the light might be, and I was afraid we should be on top of it before we could stop. But it was farther away than I thought, and a very bright light it must have been for me to catch sight of it all that distance away. And as we got closer, I could see that it was swinging slowly from side to side, a foot or so above rail level, just as if somebody was holding it at arm's length and swinging it. But it was a brighter light than any railway lantern I've ever known. Or maybe it seemed bright to me because I was afraid of running into it before I could stop."

"Did you form any idea of what the light could mean?" Arnold asked.

"I hadn't much time to form ideas, sir. My job was to get the train stopped. Something was amiss ahead, and there was the light to warn me. Well, sir, I managed to get the train in hand, and saw that I could pull up before I reached the light. And then, all at once, it changed to green, which means all clear, sir."

"How far from the light were you when this happened?"

"It's hard to say, sir. Maybe a hundred yards. Rather more, perhaps, certainly not less. So I took off the brakes, and let the steam into the cylinders again."

"Whereabout in the tunnel were you by this time?"

"Just about the middle, sir. I whistled to show that I'd seen the green light. And then I saw that the chap who was swinging it must have been standing between the up and the down lines."

"Did you see the man himself?"

"No, sir, it was too dark for that. But the light was swinging between the two sets of rails, so the man must have been standing there. And he turned off his lantern altogether just before I reached him."

"You mean that the green light disappeared?"

"That's right, sir. I tried to see the chap as I passed him, but my own steam was coming down round about the cab by then, and I couldn't see anything. And though my mate hollered, the chap didn't answer, or if he did we didn't hear him. And that's the truth, sir. It's no good telling me that there was nobody in the tunnel, for I know there was. Else how could those lights have been there?"

Arnold was evidently impressed by the driver's circumstantial description. "All right, Prentice, I believe you," he said. "You might send Haynes in here, will you? I'd like to hear what he's got to say about it."

The fireman confirmed his companion's story in every detail. Arnold did his best to find some discrepancy in the two accounts, but failed completely. Haynes was as ready to swear to the presence of the lights as Prentice had been. "And it seemed to me, sir, that the light didn't come from one of they ordinary lanterns," he added.

"What made you think that?" Arnold asked.

"Well, you see, sir, the lights was too bright, for one thing. We must have been half a mile or more away from the red light when Bob shut off steam. When he first saw it, that was, you understand. And, though there wasn't as much steam in the tunnel as usual, it was still a bit hazy. You wouldn't see an ordinary lantern as far as that. And, for another thing, the light didn't seem to shine in one direction, like a lantern does. It showed all round, like."

"And yet you couldn't see the man who was holding it?"

"No, sir, and that seemed queer to me at the time. For, if the light showed all round, it ought to have shone on him so that we could see him. At least, that's what I make out, sir."

"And you make out quite right, it seems to me. All right, Haynes, that'll do. I'm much obliged to you."

The fireman departed, and Arnold turned to Merrion. "Well, what do you make of it?" he asked.

"I don't know what to make of it," Merrion replied. "Those two fellows are telling the truth, any one could see that. They couldn't have made up a yarn like that, and stuck to it under your cross-examination. The lights were there, right enough. But what were they there for, and who showed them? We've got to have a look inside that tunnel, I can see that."

"Yes, and we've got to satisfy ourselves how much can really be seen from the signal-boxes. I've been having a look at the calendar. On Thursday the sun set at 4.11, and the moon didn't rise till after eight. The train entered the tunnel at half-past five, or very soon after. The man can't have got into the tunnel much after quarter past, if those chaps saw the lights about the middle of it. But it would be pretty dark by then. He must have managed to slip past one of the signal-boxes unobserved, whatever the station-master says."

"It's a most extraordinary business, and I don't begin to understand it. Let's see your friend the station-master, and arrange for a personally conducted tour. But I'll admit that the prospect doesn't exactly fill me with rapture."

The station-master, still sceptical, put them in charge of a ganger, and the three began to walk towards the northern end of the tunnel. The cutting leading to it began almost immediately beyond Blackdown Station, and ran through the solid chalk. The walls of the cutting were very nearly vertical, and would have afforded a precarious foothold, even to an experienced rock-climber in daylight. In the dark, the ascent or descent would have been impossible. And unless it was dark, any one attempting it would have been in full view from the platforms of Blackdown Station.

"If any one got into the tunnel from this end, they must have walked along the line from the station, the same as we are doing," said Arnold. "Well, that wouldn't be impossible in the dark. But could they have got past the signal-box unobserved? That's the point."

The signal-box, when they reached it, proved to be within a few yards of the entrance to the tunnel. The wall of the cutting had been recessed to receive it, and the box, which was fronted with glass, looked across to the opposite wall. The signalman, whom they visited, explained that at night both tracks were brightly illuminated by the lights within the box. He had himself been on duty from two to six in the afternoon on the previous Thursday. The evening had been clear, and the atmospheric conditions such that the entrance of the tunnel had been free from smoke. He was absolutely certain that nobody could have passed his box without being seen. Arnold and Merrion, seeing the conditions, were inclined to agree with him.

Then came the exploration of the tunnel itself. Up till now there had been a path beside the down line, which, though uncomfortably close to the trains as they roared past, still afforded a measure of safety. But, at the entrance of the tunnel, the path ended. Thence it was necessary to walk on the permanent way, keeping a sharp look-out for trains, taking to the down line if an up train was heard, and vice versa. Here and there within the tunnel were refuges, caves dug out of the wall in which the three of them could barely crouch. More than once they were forced to seek shelter in one of these, when both an up and down train approached them simultaneously.

The atmosphere was, in any case, positively suffocating, though the ganger assured them that conditions were exceptionally favourable. "Why, in some weathers you can't see a flare a dozen yards away," he said. "It's tricky work then, I can tell you, gentlemen. You've got to keep your wits about you, for you know the drivers can't see you any more than you can see them. And as to breathing, you've got to take a mouthful of air when you can, and think yourself lucky to get that."

They had a mild taste of this when a heavy goods train came through, steaming hard against the gradient. A torrent of red sparks poured from the funnel of the engine, and they understood Prentice's first supposition on seeing the red light. As the engine passed them, the whirl of disturbed air seemed to snatch them in an endeavour to drag them under the wheels. Then, immediately they were enveloped in a warm clinging murk of steam and sulphurous smoke. The hot cinders descended on the backs of their necks, the trucks roared and clanged past within a few inches of them. Not until the train had passed and the air had cleared a little did they venture to leave the refuge in which they had taken shelter.

Arnold and Merrion had provided themselves with powerful torches, with which they inspected the floor and sides of the tunnel. But the most careful search revealed nothing among the grime and cinders which covered everything but the rails themselves. They had asked the ganger to tell them when they reached the middle of the tunnel, but it seemed an age before he did so. And here their search became even more meticulous than before. Slowly they pursued their way, examining every square inch between the intervals of dodging the passing trains.

The ganger watched their persistence with an amused tolerance. "You're giving yourselves a lot of trouble for nothing, gentlemen," he said. "I don't care what that driver and fireman say. There was nobody in the tunnel on Thursday evening, as I know well enough. Why, how could he have got in or out? You're seeing things for yourselves, now, and it ought to be as plain to you as it is to me."

They were inclined to agree with him. And yet, unless some supernatural explanation could be imagined, how was the presence of the lights to be accounted for? That Prentice and Haynes had actually seen them, neither Arnold nor Merrion had any doubt, despite the incredulity of the local railwaymen.

Still they plodded on, and, as they did so, the atmosphere seemed to get worse, and the sulphurous fumes more suffocating. Merrion remarked upon this. "The air wasn't quite so bad just now," he said. "And yet you say we're past the middle of the tunnel, where one would expect it to be at its worst. How do you account for that?"

"It's always so," the ganger replied. "You see, there's a ventilating shaft about the middle. We're fifty or sixty yards beyond it now. The air will get worse again for a bit, then better as we get towards the southern end. Hallo, I believe your friend's found something. Look out, sir! That's the whistle of a down train coming."

Arnold had devoted his attention to the down line, while Merrion had kept his directed on the up. At the ganger's warning, he hastily stepped across to the up line. "There's something there, between the rails," he said. "Something that reflected the light of my torch. I distinctly saw it glitter. We'll have a look when this confounded train is past."

The train roared past them, and it was a minute or two before the reek which it left in its wake cleared sufficiently to allow anything to be seen. And then, between the rails of the down line, Merrion saw something glittering. Arnold went forward and picked it up. It was a curved fragment of thin red glass.

This find led to others of a similar nature. As they advanced, step by step, other fragments of glass appeared in the light of their torches. Each of these they picked up, to find that some were red and others green. It was left to Merrion to make the final discovery. Close to the side of the tunnel, and lying on the ground three or four yards apart, he found two brass electric lamp-holders, badly dented and with the porcelain interiors smashed to atoms, but each with a few inches of flexible cord still attached to it. From their comparative cleanliness it was easy to see that they had not lain in the tunnel for very long.

"Well, that settles it," said Arnold. "There are the lights that Prentice and Haynes saw, or rather the remains of them." He turned to the ganger. "How do you account for these? Do your men use red and green electric lights when they are working in here?"

The ganger shook his head. "Not that kind, anyhow," he replied. "The only way they can have got here is for somebody to have dropped them from a train. You'd be surprised if you could see some of the things that passengers do drop in tunnels."

"I dare say they drop all kinds of queer things," said Arnold. "But, all the same, I don't believe that these were dropped from a train. I believe they were brought in here by somebody, and thrown down when he had finished with them."

"Well, sir, you must have it your own way, I suppose," replied the ganger, quite unconvinced. "We'd best be moving along. Perhaps one of you gentlemen will find the chap you're after still hiding in one of the refuges."

They paid no attention to this sarcastic observation, but resumed their march in silence. But, in spite of redoubled watchfulness, they found no more. At last, a faint glimmer of daylight indicated the southern end of the tunnel. Before very long they were once more in the open air.

Merrion drew several deep breaths, cleansing his lungs of the fumes he had inhaled. "My word!" he exclaimed. "That confounded tunnel must be as near an approach to hell as human ingenuity can devise. My classics are getting a bit rusty, but wasn't it Hercules who went down into the infernal regions to rescue his pal's wife? Alcestis, that was the girl's name! I never realised before what a plucky chap he must have been. A dozen distressed damsels wouldn't tempt me into that tunnel again. And here's the other signal-box we heard about, I suppose?"

Conditions at the southern end of the tunnel were very similar to those at the northern end. A deep cutting, with vertical walls, and a signal-box commanding the entrance. Here, too, the signalman was positive that nobody could enter or leave the tunnel unobserved.

Arnold looked at his watch. It had taken them nearly two hours to traverse the two and a half miles of the tunnel.

VII

THE GANGER, TO WHOM TUNNELS WERE ALL PART OF THE DAY'S work, went back to Blackdown by the way he had come. Arnold and Merrion, however, preferred a less hazardous, if longer, route. They made their way across the fields to a neighbouring main road, where they caught a bus. They were back at Scotland Yard shortly after six o'clock.

Arnold laid upon the table the fragments which they had collected in the tunnel, and together they examined them. From their shape, it was easy to see that the bits of coloured glass were all that remained of two electric light bulbs, one red and the other green. The lamp-holders were of the ordinary type, and the flexible cord likewise. There was nothing distinctive about these.

"So there was a man in the tunnel, after all," said Arnold at last. "I can't imagine, after what we've seen this afternoon, how he got there. It's ridiculous to suppose that he bribed the signalmen not to see him. He had those two lamps with him, and he switched on the red one first, then, when the train had slowed down sufficiently, he switched on the green. He wouldn't want the train to come to a stop, for then investigations would have been made by the train-staff. He would have been found, and made to give some explanation of what he was up to."

Merrion nodded. "Those lamps prove that Prentice and Haynes are speaking the truth. If they were unshaded, they would show a light all round, instead of in one direction only, as a lantern does. And a powerful electric lamp, such as these appear to have been, would be visible a lot farther than an ordinary railway lantern. As a guess, after seeing the conditions in that infernal tunnel, I should think that to be seen at a distance of half a mile, the lamps must have been of at least a hundred candle-power each. And that raises an even bigger problem than how the chap got into the tunnel."

"Well, let's have it," said Arnold. "One problem more or less won't make much difference."

"Here you are, then. Electric lamps don't produce light of themselves. They have to be supplied with current. Where did the chap get his current from? There's no electric supply main running through the tunnel, you know."

"I'm well aware of that. The man carried a battery with him, of course. Just as we carry batteries in our torches."

Merrion shook his head. "The lamps in our torches aren't a hundred candle-power, or anything like it. Being quite small, they take very little current, and a small battery is enough to supply it. But to supply current for these lamps nothing lighter than a fair-sized motor-car battery would do. Have you ever tried carrying one of them about? They're devilish heavy, I can tell you. It would be a terrific feat to carry one into the middle of the tunnel and out again.

"Yet, by using ordinary household bulbs, this man deliberately saddled himself with the necessity for such a battery. Why did he use that kind of lamp? A couple of large-sized torches, or even one, with a movable red and green screen fitted to it, would have done just as well. By means of a lens and reflector a torch is made to give as much light as one of these lamps. But this is done by concentrating the light in one direction only. The only possible reason for using ordinary lamps, with their much greater expenditure of current, would be to obtain the advantage of the light showing all round. But, in heaven's name, why should this chap have wanted that?"

"I haven't the least idea," Arnold replied, shrugging his shoulders. "Your imagination is leading you away from the point. What reason the chap may have had for using lamps instead of torches can't possibly matter. Here are the lamps, or what's left of them. That's sufficient proof to me that the chap used them, and that he had with him a source of current from which to light them up. And when he'd done with them, he chucked them aside in the tunnel. So much is plain enough."

Merrion picked up the bits of flexible cord and examined them intently. "Our friend's proceedings strike me as bordering on the insane," he said. "He burdens himself with a cumbrous battery, when a far lighter torch would have served him equally well. When he has finished with his apparatus, he throws away the lightest part, and keeps the heaviest. For he certainly didn't leave the battery in the tunnel, or we should have found it. And he doesn't just disconnect his flexible. He breaks it violently, as you can see for yourself if you look at it."

"I'm not interested in details like that," said Arnold impatiently. "Do look at the matter sensibly, there's a good chap. We know now that Prentice and Haynes weren't imagining things when they saw those lights. Therefore a man had entered the tunnel with the definite object of slowing down the train. Why should he want to slow down the train? Tell me that."

"So that he could board it, I suppose," Merrion replied. "Look here, Arnold, have you ever climbed into an English railway carriage when it wasn't standing at a platform?"

"Yes, I climbed into that first-class coach when it was standing in the siding at Stourford yesterday morning."

"Would you have liked to have done so with a battery weighing at least fifty pounds slung round your neck, and the coach moving?"

"Oh, damn the battery!" Arnold exclaimed. "This chap did it, anyhow. You admit that his only possible reason for slowing down the train was that he could board it. What did he board it for? To get a free ride to Stourford?"

"You think that finding these lamps in the tunnel is sufficient evidence that Saxonby was murdered?"

"No, I don't. By themselves, the lamps are evidence that the driver and fireman were speaking the truth, and no more. But the fact that the train was deliberately slowed down by some unauthorised person considerably strengthens the possibility of murder. We can say now that we have reason to believe that some one got on to the train in the tunnel. We have to find that person, and discover whether he knows anything about Sir Wilfred's death."

"That's very clearly put," said Merrion approvingly. "But, you know, all the difficulties which we discussed yesterday still remain. How did the man know that Saxonby was alone, or which compartment he occupied? For he must have entered the train by that particular compartment. You see why. All the others were occupied, and his sudden entry into any of them from the tunnel would have caused at least a mild surprise. Then, what became of him? You'll have to interview those twenty-four first-class passengers, I'm afraid."

"Marden, down at Stourford, is rounding them up for me. They all live round about there, as it happens. I shall have to go down and see him to-morrow, and hear what he's done. Care to come?"

Merrion agreed, readily enough. The problem fascinated him, since every possible solution presented apparently insuperable difficulties. He had seen for himself the impossibility of entering or leaving the tunnel unobserved. Yet somebody must have entered it, or how could the presence of the lamps be explained? That they had been casually thrown from a passing train was too fantastic a theory to be entertained for a moment.

And how had the man left the tunnel? In the train, or on foot? The former seemed most likely. He had taken Saxonby's ticket, and hid in the lavatory till the train got to Stourford. That was it, undoubtedly.

As for the battery, he must have thrown it out of the window, somewhere between the tunnel and Stourford. Since nobody had been allowed to get out of the coach without giving a name and address, it ought to be possible to trace him.

Merrion laid this reasoning before Arnold on their way to Stourford next morning. The inspector saw the force of it, and it was evidently in his mind when they met Marden at the police station. For his first question was, "Have you traced all those twenty-four passengers, Mr. Marden?"

"Every one of them," Marden replied. "It wasn't difficult for they are all local people, and there's nothing in any way suspicious about any of them."

"Yes, but are you quite sure that they all got into the train at Cannon Street? That's the point."

"As sure as any one can be. They have all given accounts of their movements, which can be checked. But the curious thing is that there ought to be twenty-five of them, instead of twenty-four."

"What do you mean, Mr. Marden?" Arnold asked eagerly.

"Why, so far as I can make out, there was one passenger who got on to the train at Cannon Street who wasn't in the coach when it reached here. I expect you'll like to hear the story at first hand. If so, I'll take you to see a couple of ladies who live close here. Mrs. Clutsam a widow, and her daughter."

Marden took them to a fine old house on the outskirts of the town, and introduced them to Mrs. Clutsam. She was quite ready to repeat her story, and called her daughter to support her.

"We had been up to London for the day to do some shopping," she said. "Now that they've reduced the price of day tickets, we always travel first. It's so much more comfortable, and it isn't a very great extravagance. We got to Cannon Street about ten minutes to five, and looked for seats in the train. We never go in smoking carriages if we can help it, for they always seem more crowded. And we found a non-smoker, with only one old gentleman in it.

"He was sitting in the corner seat next to the corridor, facing the engine, and he had put a newspaper in the opposite seat. He kept looking out on to the platform, and then at his watch. He was obviously expecting somebody, we could see that. He got very perturbed as the time came for the train to start, but nobody came. And when the train began to move, we heard him mutter, 'Dear, dear, she's missed it again!' Didn't we, Betty?"

"Yes, we certainly did," replied Miss Clutsam. "The poor old boy seemed very much annoyed, or disappointed, perhaps. But after a minute or two he took his paper from the opposite seat, and began to read it."

"He read it for quite a long time," her mother chimed in. "I noticed that he seemed very nearsighted, for he held it close to his eyes. Then, after a while, he took out a cigarette-case, chose a cigarette, and was just going to light it when he remembered that he was in a non-smoker. He held the unlighted cigarette and looked at it in such a funny way that I couldn't help laughing. And then I said to him, 'Please light your cigarette. We don't mind a bit.' Didn't I, Betty?"

"I don't think he liked being laughed at," replied Miss Clutsam. "He mentioned something about not thinking of inconveniencing us, and that he could easily find a seat in a smoking carriage. And with that he got up and tottered off."

"We were passing through a station at the time. Blackdown, I think it must have been. And we never saw him again."

"I wonder if you could describe him, Mrs. Clutsam?" Arnold asked.

"Oh, I should think he must have been about seventy. He was wearing a heavy dark brown overcoat, and he had a short grey beard.

I couldn't see much of his face, for he held the paper so close to it. But it seemed to me very much wrinkled."

"He had a hooked nose, and reminded me of a parrot," said Miss Clutsam.

"He stooped as he walked, and seemed very tottery on his legs. I told mother that it was a shame to have laughed at him, since it had driven him out of the carriage."

Neither of the ladies could add anything to this. The two inspectors and Merrion left the house and returned to the police-station. "Now, I'll carry on the story," said Marden. "As soon as I heard about this old man with the short grey beard, I went round the rest of the passengers again. None of them had seen him. Neither he nor anybody else had entered any of the compartments after the train had left Cannon Street. No stranger, I mean. Three or four of the passengers had left their seats to go to the lavatory, but they had all returned to them.

"Then I went to the railway station, and questioned our friend Cutbush and his merry men. Cutbush is perfectly certain that nobody answering to that description was in the coach when it arrived here. Being thorough by nature, he had ascertained that there was nobody in either of the lavatories. The ticket-collector is equally certain that the old man with the short grey beard did not pass the barrier. Having been here for many years, he knew nearly all the passengers by sight, and he is quite certain that this man was not among them. Now, what about it?"

Arnold shook his head. "It beats me," he replied. "It seems to me that very remarkable things happen on this line of yours. I'll tell you what Mr. Merrion and I found yesterday."

Marden listened with interest. "So there was a man in Blackdown Tunnel, after all!" he exclaimed. "That's two men we've got to look for, now. But where can the old chap with the beard have got to? He can't have got out of the train when it slowed down in the tunnel, surely? You heard what Miss Clutsam said about his being tottery."

"I shouldn't wonder if that, and the beard, and the wrinkles and all were put on," Arnold replied. "This business will take years from my life. It's impossible for anybody to get in or out of that tunnel without being seen. Yet, on Thursday evening, people seem to have gone in and out at their own sweet will. From what I can make out one must have gone in, and two came out. But how? Merrion, your imagination has never been known to fail. Tell me how?"

But Merrion shook his head. "I wish I could," he replied. "Unless they had the cloak of the fairy stories, which made them invisible. But I think we should be pretty safe in assuming now that these extraordinary happenings had some connection with Saxonby's death."

"Meaning that Sir Wilfred was murdered by the man with the beard?" said Arnold. "Well, we've got to try and find the chap, I suppose. But it won't be any too easy. He was obviously disguised, and we haven't the slightest idea what the real man looks like.

"What do we know about him? Precious little. He got into the five o'clock from Cannon Street on Thursday. That job about expecting some one to join him was rather neat. It gave him the chance of watching for Sir Wilfred, and seeing which compartment he got into. Just before the train reached the tunnel, he left his own compartment, and walked along the corridor. We must suppose he entered Sir Wilfred's compartment, and if so he must have had a railway key. He shot him, and put the pistol under the seat where it was certain to be found. Then, when the train had slowed down sufficiently, he dropped off it. We've got to work on that theory, I think. By the way, how did the inquest go off yesterday, Mr. Marden?"

"Adjourned for further evidence," Marden replied. "I think the coroner was a bit surprised when we made the suggestion. Nobody about here has any doubt that Sir Wilfred shot himself."

At this moment the telephone bell rang, and Marden answered it. He held a short conversation, then turned to the others. "That was Miss Olivia Saxonby," he said. "She wants to drive over here and see me at once. A matter of some importance, she said. I told her to come along. Perhaps you gentlemen would like to be present at the interview?"

"Thanks," replied Arnold. "We may as well. Have you any idea what she wants to see you about?"

"None whatever. I sent Sir Wilfred's clothes and things to Mavis Court this morning. That may have something to do with it."

While awaiting their visitor, they discussed the new aspects of the case. The vital point now was to discover the identity of the man with the beard. But they had reached no conclusion when Miss Saxonby was announced. She showed no trace of excitement, or, indeed, of any other emotion. Having been accommodated with a chair, she produced a wallet, which Arnold recognised as the one which had been found in the dead man's pocket, and laid it on the table. "That didn't belong to Uncle Wilfred," she said.

"But it was the one which was found in his pocket, Miss Saxonby," Marden replied. "How can you be sure that it did not belong to him?"

"Perhaps I expressed myself badly. It may have belonged to him, though I have never seen it before. It certainly is not the wallet which he took with him on Thursday morning, though, it is exactly like it."

"Are you sure that it is not the same, Miss Saxonby?"

"Quite sure. Uncle Wilfred had a wallet exactly like this, which was given to him by my cousin Dick last Christmas. Since then he always used it, carrying it about with him in his pocket.

"On Wednesday afternoon, at tea time, he took it out and showed me where the silk lining had gone torn. I told him that I thought I could stitch it up for him. He emptied the wallet, and gave it to me. I mended it as best I could, and gave it back to him. As you see, the lining is of light blue silk. I hadn't any thread exactly that colour, and had to use a darker shade, which made the stitches show.

"Just before he left Mavis Court on Thursday morning, he took his wallet from his pocket to give me some money, and I noticed the stitches then. So the wallet which he took to London was the one which I had mended. If you look at this one, you will see that though the lining is frayed in places, it is not torn, and there are no stitches in it."

This was certainly the case, but the significance of the fact was not immediately apparent. It was left to Merrion to ask the next question. "Do you happen to know where your cousin bought the wallet which he gave to your uncle?"

"I haven't the slightest idea," she replied. "You can ask him when he gets back from America."

"You found all the rest of Sir Wilfred's possessions correct, Miss Saxonby?" Arnold asked.

"So far as I know. But, of course, I can't tell exactly what he had in his pockets or his attaché-case when he went up to London."

She rose, and Marden escorted her from the room. Merrion smiled. "If she's telling the truth, and if Saxonby was murdered, I believe that we're beginning to get an inkling of the motive," he said.

VIII

IT WAS NOT UNTIL HE AND ARNOLD WERE ALONE, IN THE train going back to London, that Merrion deigned to explain himself.

"If that isn't the wallet which Saxonby took with him to London, where did it come from?" he asked. "You will have observed that it does not appear to be new. Both the leather and the silk lining are worn. That, I think, disposes of our theory. Saxonby's aesthetic taste may have been displeased by the stitches put in by his niece. He might have bought another wallet to replace his own, while he was in London. But then he would have bought a new one. And it is in the highest degree improbable that he possessed two exactly similar wallets, which could only be distinguished by the lining of one of them being torn.

"May I remind you of the railway ticket and the letter from Mrs. Wardour? Their disappearance has puzzled us, and now that we believe that a man left the train in the tunnel, instead of boarding it, my ingenious theory to account for the ticket won't do. To these missing articles we have to add Saxonby's wallet. Do you mind telling me again what were the contents of the wallet found in his pocket?"

Arnold referred to his note-book. "A few of Saxonby's visiting cards, a book of stamps, with two or three torn out, three five-pound notes, seven one-pound notes, and two ten-shilling notes."

"Nothing, in fact, particularly intimate. Nothing that anybody might have procured for himself. Even the visiting cards could have been copied from one given to somebody by Saxonby. But we have reason to believe that, when Saxonby started on his journey home, his wallet contained also his daughter's letter and his ticket. Are you beginning to see daylight?"

"No, I'm blest if I am," Arnold replied. "I haven't the least idea what you're driving at."

"Very well. Now, suppose that Saxonby's wallet, which we will call Number One, contained, besides all these things, some valuable document. A certain person decides to possess himself of that document. With that end in view he works out a scheme for murdering Saxonby in Blackdown Tunnel, in such a way as to make it appear that he committed suicide.

"The very essence of his scheme is speed. He dare not remain in Saxonby's compartment an instant longer than he can help, for fear that somebody passing along the corridor may see him. He must choose the moment when the train is travelling at its minimum speed. Then he must enter the compartment, shoot his victim, secure the document, and get off the train. And all this must be done within a few seconds.

"This rapid programme allowed no time for looking through wallet number one, which may have contained a quantity of letters and papers. Nor could he just take the wallet and leave nothing in its place. Its absence would arouse suspicion as soon as the body was found. So he evolves rather a neat scheme. He provides himself with a second wallet, which we will call number two, exactly similar, so far as he knows, to number one. And in this wallet he puts things such as Saxonby habitually carried about him. Visiting cards, a book of stamps, and a fair amount of money. What he can't put in is the return half of a railway ticket to Stourford, and Mrs. Wardour's letter. The ticket, because it was a day return, and he would have had to purchase it at Stourford, and the letter, for obvious reasons. Wallet number two he had all ready with its contents. All he had to do when he had killed Saxonby was to take number one, and put number two in its place."

"I don't understand..." Arnold protested, but Merrion cut him short. "Of course you don't. Nor do I, yet. But I'll bet you I'm right. Saxonby was murdered by somebody who wanted to secure something that he had in his wallet. If that's the case, we can deduce quite a lot of things about that somebody. He was intimately acquainted with Saxonby, to such an extent as to know the exact appearance of his wallet. And that seems to me to show a remarkable degree of intimacy. We've known one another several years. I habitually carry a wallet, which you must have seen me produce a hundred times. Could you go and buy one exactly like it?"

Arnold shook his head. "I remember that it is brown, and made of crocodile skin. But I couldn't tell you what colour the lining is, for instance."

"Exactly. Now, what else do we know about the supposed murderer? He was aware that Saxonby would be carrying the valuable document, or whatever it was, on Thursday evening. And people don't carry a thing like that about with them all day and every day. They keep it in a place of safety. Another suggestion, I think, that Saxonby's murderer knew a great deal about his victim's private affairs."

"That's all very well," said Arnold. "But you are building up a theory upon a supposition that is pure guess-work. You have assumed the existence of this valuable document without, so far as I can see, the slightest grounds for doing so."

"Not altogether. You may remember that we considered Saxonby's actions, and agreed that they fitted in very well with the theory of suicide. He sent the members of his family to a distance, for instance, and gave a large tip to Turner for the privilege of having a carriage to himself. We have now abandoned the theory of suicide, but the actions remain. Can we find, supposing now that Saxonby was murdered, any other theory to account for them? I think we can.

"Suppose that Saxonby knew that on Thursday last he would receive an article, X. I won't call it a valuable document, if you think that is assuming too much. X was of such a nature as to be carried in his wallet. It was of considerable value, intrinsic or otherwise. It would be delivered to him at his office, and would need to be conveyed to Mavis Court. Its receipt must not be known to Saxonby's son or daughter, both of whom are directors of Wigland and Bunthorne, and might be in the offices at any time. What would Saxonby do? Why, just exactly what we know him to have done. He disposes of his possibly inquisitive family, on different pretexts. You said, I think, that the secretary, Torrance, happened to be in Manchester last Thursday. I shouldn't wonder if it turned out that he went there at Saxonby's suggestion.

"You also said that Saxonby had a visitor, who gave the name of Yates, and was a stranger to the staff. Was he the man who brought X? In any case, we will suppose that Saxonby obtained this mysterious object in the course of the day, and put it in wallet number one. When the time came to go home, his chief concern was lest his pocket should be picked. So he takes all precautions. Instead of walking to Cannon Street, he sends for a taxi, a thing, apparently, which he has never been known to do before. Arrived at the station, he secures, at considerable expense, a carriage to himself, and sees that the door is locked. He fancies then that he is secure. He can't be expected to divine the deep-laid schemes of the old man with the short grey beard."

"Upon my word, Merrion, your imagination gets more vivid every day!" Arnold exclaimed. "Don't let any doubting attitude on my part cramp your style. Can't you deduce the identity of the murderer in the same brilliant fashion?"

"Do you know, I'm almost tempted to make a guess? You don't happen to have that automatic in your pocket by any chance, do you?"

"No, I left it at the Yard for the experts to report upon."

"You said it had initials engraved upon it. Can you describe them?"

"Yes, W.S., in rather ornate letters in the form of a monogram."

"A monogram! Then how do you know that the initials are W.S. and not S.W.?"

"For the simple and fairly obvious reason that Sir Wilfred's initials were W.S."

Merrion smiled. "Saxonby's daughter married a Major Wardour. Have you ever inquired what his Christian name is? What would you say if it turned out to be Samuel?"

"Dash it all, that's going too far!" Arnold exclaimed. "I can swallow a good deal, but not that. There isn't the slightest reason to suspect Major Wardour. Besides, he's in the South of France, or was when Sir Wilfred was killed."

"So we are told. And, since at present there isn't the slightest reason to suspect anybody in particular, we may as well begin with Wardour. Let's see how he fits in. I've shown you how the murderer must have been somebody with an intimate knowledge of Saxonby. Wardour, as his son-in-law, may be supposed to have that knowledge. There seems to be some sort of trouble brewing between Wardour and his wife, in which, apparently, Saxonby took his daughter's side. The two men may have been on bad terms in consequence. If I were you, I'd try to find out rather more about Wardour than you know at present."

Arnold grunted. "I've got to find out a lot more about several people, it seems to me," he replied. "Your suggestions are stimulating, my friend, but for the present I find them a bit bewildering. I'd rather stick to plain facts. As I see it, this is pretty much what happened.

"A certain individual was already seated in the train at the time when Sir Wilfred secured his solitary compartment. This individual appeared to be elderly, bearded, and somewhat decrepit. Until the train started, he kept a careful watch upon the platform. To explain this, he deliberately gave Mrs. Clutsam and her daughter the impression that he was expecting somebody to join him. Just before the train entered the tunnel, he left the compartment.

"I think we may assume that he was elaborately disguised. The next question is, what became of him? He did not enter any of the compartments occupied by the surviving first-class passengers. He may have entered Sir Wilfred's compartment, but he was not there when Turner looked in, at which time the train was gathering speed again. He cannot have left the first-class coach by unlocking one of the doors at the end of the corridor, for Turner and his assistant were approaching the coach from opposite directions, and one or other must have seen him.

"I can think of only two possibilities. He may have gone into one of the lavatories, and there removed his disguise. Later, he may have gone along the train, and taken a seat in one of the thirds, whose occupants were not questioned. Or he may have left the train as it slowed down in the tunnel. Since it was slowed down intentionally by some unauthorised person, that seems to me the most likely theory."

Merrion nodded. "So it does to me. And subsequently two men, carrying a heavy battery between them, left the tunnel without being spotted. And that seems to me to need a devil of a lot of explanation."

"Explanation or no explanation, they must have left it. They weren't there yesterday afternoon, as we know well enough. And I think we may take it that they weren't there when the railwaymen looked through the tunnel on Friday morning. Now, people don't hold up trains just for fun, at least not in this country. Nor do they jump off them in tunnels just because they feel they'd like to stretch their legs a bit. There must have been some very good reason for these happenings. One naturally concludes that the shooting of Sir Wilfred constituted this reason.

"But, as you probably realise as well as I do, there is no conclusive evidence to prove that the man with the beard was the murderer. We don't know that he entered Sir Wilfred's compartment and shot him. We only believe that he had the opportunity of doing so. And as for your motive, the wish to secure the object X, that's pure guess-work."

"It's rather more than that, if it's correct that the wallets were interchanged," said Merrion thoughtfully. "You've got the numbers of those five-pound notes, I suppose? It's a very faint hope, but there's just the chance that you may be able to trace them."

"Yes, I've got the numbers. Hallo, here we are at that confounded tunnel again! Well, I'd rather go through it in the train than the way we did yesterday."

"So would I. I thought I was going to be suffocated before we got half-way through. Half-way through? By Gad, I believe I've got it!"

"Got what?" Arnold demanded.

"The essential brainwave. No, I'm not going into details now. It may be one of those flights of my imagination which don't come off somehow. What are you doing to-morrow morning?"

"I meant to take the day off, but I'm not sure now that I can."

"Oh, yes, you can. I'll show you a way of combining business with pleasure. We'll take an early train to Blackdown, and then go hiking together. Oh, yes, we will. It'll do you all the good in the world. Besides, there are some very good pubs in those parts, I believe. So we'll take it as settled."

IX

ARNOLD ALLOWED HIMSELF TO BE PERSUADED. HE KNEW BY experience that Merrion never acted from mere caprice. There was also some good, if sometimes imaginative reason, for what he did.

So the pair of them arrived at Blackdown station about ten o'clock on Monday morning, and avoiding the station-master walked into the town. Here they took the main road leading southwards, and followed it for rather more than a mile. On reaching a signpost, Merrion consulted a map which he had brought with him. They turned to the right, along a secondary road, which carried comparatively little traffic. Some distance along this, they came to a grassy lane, which wandered off through a wood. After another glance at his map, Merrion decided that they would take this. They passed through the wood, and emerged upon an open expanse of pastureland. Merrion stopped, and pointed straight in front of him. "See that?" he exclaimed triumphantly.

Arnold looked in the required direction. A few hundred yards from where they stood was a cylindrical brick structure, about six feet in diameter and eight feet high, not unlike a factory chimney cut off short just above the base. The suggestion was heightened by the fact that a feather of whitish smoke was floating lazily from the top. The inspector looked at it without interest. "That thing that's smoking over there?" he replied. "Yes, I see it. What is it? A lime-kiln, or something?"

"Lime-kiln!" Merrion retorted scornfully. "Don't you remember walking through the tunnel on Saturday? And when I remarked to the ganger that the atmosphere seemed a trifle less poisonous towards the middle, he said that was because there was a ventilating shaft there. Well, we're just about over the middle of the tunnel now, and that's the top of the shaft. The smoke you see comes up from the tunnel beneath. Now, let's go and have a look at it."

To do so, they had only to follow the lane which ran within a few feet of the shaft. Merrion looked at this thoughtfully. "I wish we'd thought of bringing a ladder," he said. "Never mind, there are one or two holes in the brickwork. Enough to give me a foothold, I think. Lend me your back a moment, will you?"

With Arnold's aid he scrambled up the side of the shaft, and perched himself on the top, with his legs dangling over the edge. He sat there for so long in silence that the inspector became impatient. "Are you going to stop up there for the rest of the day?" he asked.

"Shut up, I'm listening," replied Merrion sharply. And it was not for several minutes that he spoke again.

"It's all right," he said at last. "It works perfectly. Sitting up here I can hear the whistle of the trains as they enter the tunnel, and I'm beginning to be able to distinguish the direction from which they are coming. The roar is faint at first, then becomes louder as the train approaches the shaft. The noise is quite different as it passes under the shaft, more like a rattle. Then the roar begins again, and dies away as the train proceeds towards the other end of the tunnel. That's all I want to know to begin with. Lend me a hand down, will you?"

Arnold did so. "Listening to trains isn't a hobby of mine," he said. "Since you appear to be satisfied, let's see if we can't find a decent pub where we can have a drink."

"You'll have to curb your thirst for a little longer, I'm afraid," Merrion replied. "Look here, on the grass between the lane and the shaft. See that track? Made by a biggish car or a light lorry, unless I'm greatly mistaken. And I think these are the wheel-marks of a smaller and lighter car too. Neither of these tracks are many days old. Come and have a look at them for yourself."

"Yes, I see the tracks all right," said Arnold. "What about them?"

"Sit down here, on the leeward side of the stack, and light your pipe. What has been our chief difficulty with regard to the man or men in the tunnel?"

"Why, how they got in or out unobserved."

"Right. Well, this shaft is the way out of that difficulty. Let me explain how the trick was worked. Because we found those lamps in the tunnel, we jumped to the conclusion that there must have been a man down there to work them. But that's just where we were wrong. They were worked from up here.

"There were two men concerned, A and B. A was the man with the beard, B his confederate. B arrived here some time before half-past five in a car. I don't understand why there should be two sets of tracks, but that's a detail. He had with him in the car the battery that puzzled me so much, and the two lamps, each attached to a considerable length of flexible cord, on each of which, at the battery end, was a switch.

"He ran the car up against the shaft. I expect that it was a saloon and that by getting on to the roof he could overlook the top of the shaft. And I also expect that he had made his observations beforehand, and knew pretty well what he was about. He had probably used a lead-line, and knew the distance from the top of the shaft to the floor of the tunnel.

"He got everything ready, then waited till he heard the whistle of Saxonby's train as it entered the tunnel. Then he lowered his lamps, so that they hung by the flexible cords, and switched on the red lamp. He could tell pretty well by the sound what was happening below. He would hear the train slowing up, and when he judged it had done so sufficiently, he switched off the red lamp and switched on the green.

This bears out what Prentice and Haynes told us. The lamps swung slowly across the tunnel, between the two sets of rails. That's just what they would do if they were suspended from here.

"As the train gathered way again, B switched off the green, and started to haul up his lamps. But he wasn't quite quick enough. The engine caught them, smashed them to pieces, and broke the flexible cord. The men on the engine would see or hear nothing of that. It is too dark in the tunnel, and far too noisy. The impact threw the remains of the lamps to where we found them, which, you will remember, was some yards to the southward of the middle of the tunnel.

"Meanwhile, A had jumped off the train and made his way to the bottom of the shaft. How did he know when he had got there, you ask? Because he had a torch, which he kept pointing upwards, instead of downwards, as we did. He then calls up to B, who lowers a rope-ladder. A swarms up it, the rope-ladder is raised, and there you are."

"This time I really believe you've hit the nail on the head," said Arnold approvingly. "Your theory certainly clears up the difficulties. But I don't much like the rope-ladder part. A rope-ladder of any length is a confoundedly bulky thing to carry about. And heavy, too, for that matter."

"To be quite frank, I'm not in love with the rope-ladder, either. When I was up there just now, I looked for some place where the top end could be fixed, and couldn't find one. However, I'm pretty sure that A must have left the tunnel by the shaft, rope-ladder or no rope-ladder."

Arnold stood up and looked about him. "This confounded country seems utterly deserted," he said. "I shouldn't wonder if that car drove up and away again without anybody seeing it."

"We mustn't be too pessimistic. There must be a cottage or a farm or something somewhere. Suppose we follow this lane for a bit, and see where it leads to?"

They went on for about half a mile, and then, upon rounding a shoulder of the downs, came to a small farmhouse. An elderly man of benevolent aspect was working in the yard, and Merrion addressed him. "Can you tell us where this lane leads to?" he asked.

The man looked up and gave them a friendly smile. "Well, sir, 'tis a funny old lane, and no mistake," he replied. "It don't rightly lead nowhere, properly speaking. Just through the farm here, and out again to the road, half a mile beyond."

"Then you don't get much traffic along here, I suppose?"

"There's nobody comes along but the few folk what wants to get to the farm. Barring now and then somebody who's out for a nice walk, same as you might be, or what has lost his way and turned along the lane by mistake. There was one of them last Thursday."

"A car, do you mean?" Merrion asked casually.

"Aye, one of them little cars like overgrown prams. Bloke what was driving it turned in at the end of the lane. Said he wanted to get to Little Hazelbury. But the turning to Little Hazelbury is nigh on a mile beyond the lane, as I told him."

"Did you see him turn into the lane?"

"No, for I'd have set him right if I had, wouldn't I? 'Twas later on that I saw him, when he'd got as far as the shaft, and his car wouldn't go any further. It chanced that I was out that way, looking for a young heifer that had strayed. And I saw the car and the bloke standing by it."

"By Jove!" Merrion exclaimed. "I wonder if that was my friend Jones? He told me that his car had broken down somewhere in these parts, one day last week. What did he look like?"

"Elderly gentleman, with a short grey beard and walked with a stoop. I can't say that I took any particular notice of him. I went up to him and asked him if the car wouldn't go, and he said that he thought the magneto had broken down. That's when he told me that he was bound for Little Hazelbury."

"Poor old Jones! He's always in trouble with that bus of his. Did he manage to get her going again?"

"No. He fiddled about for a bit, and then said that he would have to find a garage and get them to send some one out. He said he'd walk back to the main road, where he could pick up a bus to take him into Blackdown. I told him it wouldn't do to leave the car where it was, as it was right in the middle of the lane, and nothing couldn't get by. He said he wasn't strong enough to move it by himself, so I lent him a hand, and we pushed it on to the grass, right beside the old shaft. And then he went off, though any one could see that he wasn't much good at walking."

"No, the poor old chap suffers terribly from rheumatism. It must have taken him a long time to walk to the main road. What time was this, by the way?"

"Somewhere round about twelve o'clock in the morning. And the chaps from the garage didn't hurry themselves about getting here. It was nigh on dark when I saw one of they breakdown lorries coming along. You'll know what I mean, sir. One of them things with a crane and tackle in them, so they can hoist a car up."

"I know them," Merrion replied. "Did Jones come with the lorry?"

"I couldn't say. I was too far off to see. I was just on my way back to get my tea. I saw the lorry drive up to where the car was standing, and then I went on. They were some time messing about, for it was well past half-past five when I heard them go off."

"You didn't see them go?"

"No. I was back here, you see. And I wouldn't have heard them, neither, but that it was a still evening."

Merrion chatted with the man for a little longer, then he and Arnold went on their way.

Merrion was delighted with what he had heard. "Now we know how the dodge was worked," he said. "We've got a pair of pretty clever rogues to deal with, my friend. A breakdown lorry! I never thought of that. So that disposes of the difficulty of the rope-ladder."

"Yes, it could easily be carried on a lorry," Arnold replied.

"It could, but it wouldn't be necessary. Don't you see? The lorry was fitted with a crane, as our rustic friend expressly stated. Right. B runs the lorry up against the shaft, and swings the crane over the top of it. When he hears A's signal from below, he lowers a rope with a bowline at the end of it. A puts his foot in the bowline, B sets the crane to work, and up comes A, like truth out of a well. Simple, neat and efficient. Now we'd better make our way to Blackdown, and see if we can't find a pub on the way."

They found a pub, at which they refreshed themselves. And during the remainder of their walk they discussed how the two men, A and B, were to be run to earth.

"It's all very well to know, or at all events to have made a pretty good guess, how they worked it," said Merrion. "But their methods were so thorough that I'm afraid there is very little chance of tracing either the small car or the lorry. The small car was probably towed for a short distance, say to the end of the lane. Then, I have no doubt, the magneto recovered miraculously, and the car and the lorry went off in different directions. And by that time it was quite dark."

"I expect you're right," Arnold replied. "As a matter of routine, I shall have to get in touch with the local police, and get them to make inquiries at the garages round about."

"Yes, you'll have to do that, of course. Meanwhile, let's see if we can disentangle their movements a bit. The elderly gentleman with the short grey beard, seen by the farmer, is obviously the same man whom Mrs. and Miss Clutsam saw in the train. The one we have called A, in fact. He turned up at the shaft in a small car about twelve o'clock on Thursday. After his conversation with the farmer, he hobbled off towards the main road. But I don't suppose he hobbled far. I expect he took off all or part of his disguise, and stepped it pretty briskly for the rest of the way. And you may bet that he didn't go near a garage.

"We lose sight of him for a bit. But he must have gone to London, for we hear of him again at Cannon Street, shortly before the departure of the five o'clock train. He disappears again just before the train enters Blackdown Tunnel. And nobody appears to have seen him since. But I think we can assume, with every confidence, that B hoisted him out of the tunnel with the aid of his crane. Where he may be now, goodness only knows.

"We know considerably less about B. We only know that he existed, from the evidence of the lights and the breakdown lorry. Somebody must have worked the one, and driven the other. A couldn't have done that, since he was in the train. We have no description of B, since we have found nobody who saw him. He is, in fact, merely an accomplice, since A was undoubtedly the murderer. But all the same, if we could find out who B was, we should very soon learn A's identity. It's like one of those double-barrelled equations, when as soon as you know the value of x, you can find the value of y, and vice versa."

"There's one thing in our favour," said Arnold. "This isn't just a casual murder, which might have been committed by anybody. Two men put their heads together, and worked out the details in advance."

"Well in advance. The breakdown lorry had to be arranged for. The peculiarities of the shaft had to be studied. Wallet number two had to be procured. The pistol had to be obtained, and if the initials were not already on it, they had to be engraved. All these things would take time."

They walked on for some little way in silence, each busy with his own thoughts. "Well, you've certainly shown me something this morning," said Arnold at last. "I should never have thought of that confounded shaft. Your imagination put you on the right track there. Perhaps the rest of your theories are not so far-fetched as I was inclined to think them yesterday. Anyhow, I'll adopt them as something to begin on, if you don't mind."

"You're welcome. I don't claim any copyright in them. Might one ask what line you are going to take?"

"I'm going to begin with the pistol, which, after all, is the most tangible clue we've got. By the time I get back to the Yard the experts ought to have found out all about it. Their report may give us a clue. Then I'll tackle the wallets and their contents. Finally, I'll try to find out whether Sir Wilfred did actually receive something of value, your object X, on Thursday. It may be possible to trace the man who called upon him that day, giving the name of Yates."

"That seems pretty sound," Merrion replied. "I can't offer to help you, for I must get back home this evening. But I could come up again in a day or two should you happen to want me. Just one thing. Don't forget Major Wardour."

They travelled back to Charing Cross together, and there they parted.

X

AS SOON AS ARNOLD REACHED SCOTLAND YARD HE EMBARKED upon the programme which he had outlined to Merrion. The firearms experts had completed their examination of the pistol found in the railway compartment, and at the inspector's request their spokesman joined him in the former's room, bringing the pistol with him.

"It is a very common type of self-loading pistol," he said. "It is not correct to call it an automatic. An automatic, properly speaking, is a weapon which keeps on firing as long as the trigger is pressed, until the magazine is exhausted. This fires a single shot when the trigger is pressed, loads a second when it is released, fires this when the trigger is pressed a second time, and so on.

"Its calibre is .22, and the magazine holds six cartridges. It is of Belgian manufacture, and was made last year. We have communicated with the makers, giving them the number, which you can see stamped upon it. They believe, but cannot be absolutely certain, that it formed part of a consignment delivered to one of their agents in Brussels. In any case, they are certain that it was not exported by them to this country.

"When it was delivered to us it had recently been discharged, and had not been cleaned since. Its internal condition shows that it has seen some service. Several rounds have been fired from it, as can be seen by examination of the mechanism. But it has been in the hands of somebody who took the trouble to look after it. He had cleaned and oiled it after use, except on the occasion of the last shot fired from it."

"He hadn't much time for cleaning and oiling on that occasion," remarked Arnold grimly. "It is pretty certain, then, that this pistol was purchased in Belgium?"

"Apparently. And within the last twelve months or so, if our information from the makers is correct. In any case, not many of these small self-loaders are sold in this country now. They aren't very much good, except at very short ranges. And a man needs a fair amount of practice before he can do any very accurate shooting with them, even then."

"This pistol would kill a man at point-blank range, if the bullet went through some vital part?"

"Oh, yes. Even a .22 calibre bullet will do a lot of damage. And this particular pistol takes a long cartridge, which means that its muzzle velocity is fairly high. It is certainly capable of inflicting a fatal wound at several yards."

"Did you examine the cartridges as well?"

"Yes. There were two packets of them, one labelled 'Found in magazine' the other 'Found in Sir W.S.'s office.' On comparing the cartridges from these two packets, we found them exactly similar. In fact, I think it is safe to say that they came from the same batch. There is no indication of the maker of the cartridges, but we have formed the opinion, from certain peculiarities which they exhibit, that they are of Belgian origin. One might suppose that they were bought at the same time and place as the pistol."

"You can't say definitely that they were, I suppose?"

"No. But they and the pistol are of the same country of origin, and approximately the same date. Rather suggestive, isn't it?"

"Yes. You're pretty certain that both packets of cartridges come from the same batch? That's rather an important point, as it happens."

"As sure as one can be about anything of the kind."

When his informant had gone, leaving him alone, Arnold frowned. The report of the firearms expert confirmed everything which he had originally conjectured for himself. The pistol had been bought in Belgium, within the last twelve months. Sir Wilfred had visited Belgium during the previous summer. It was rather curious that there was a slight conflict of opinion as to his reasons for doing so. Miss Saxonby believed that he had gone on business. Torrance was certain that business had had nothing to do with his journey. That, however, was a minor consideration.

The cartridges had, in all probability, been bought at the same time and place as the pistol. Those found in Sir Wilfred's filing cabinet were exactly similar to those extracted from the magazine of the pistol. Nobody but Sir Wilfred himself had access to that cabinet. Surely this suggested that he had bought the pistol and cartridges during his visit to Belgium? Further, that since his purchase he had kept the pistol and cartridges in the cabinet. Finally, that he had loaded the pistol and taken it with him on the previous Thursday afternoon.

Why should he have done so? Arnold's original answer had been, because he intended to commit suicide. But the light which had been thrown upon the incident of the tunnel had rather discredited the theory of suicide. Suppose he had not intended to commit suicide, what other reason could he have had for taking the pistol on that particular evening? Arnold remembered Merrion's fantastic theory about the mysterious object which he had called X. If Sir Wilfred had been taking some object of value home with him, was it not possible that he had put the pistol in his pocket as a defence in case of attack?

Quite possible. A very natural precaution. But the attack had actually taken place, it appeared, and Sir Wilfred had been killed with the very weapon which was to afford him protection. How was that to be explained? Did the murderer snatch the pistol from his victim's pocket and shoot him with it? Arnold saw at once the difficulties in the way of this theory. How could the murderer know that Sir Wilfred was carrying a loaded pistol in, say, his right-hand overcoat pocket?

But the second difficulty was not so easily brushed aside. Sir Wilfred, according to Merrion's theory, had determined to take every precaution against robbery. The taxi, the care to secure a compartment to himself. He had, presumably, remained on the alert, even while in the train. It was ridiculous to suppose that he would have allowed a stranger entering his compartment to snatch his weapon and shoot him with it. He would have been far more likely to draw the pistol himself and threaten the intruder with it. Had he done so, and been overpowered? The sound of the struggle might not have been overheard above the roar of the tunnel. But one would have expected the compartment to show signs of it. And of such signs there had been none.

Another explanation passed through the inspector's mind. Sir Wilfred would have taken the alarm at the intrusion of a stranger, but not, perhaps, of somebody he knew. It was just possible that the elderly man with the short grey beard was known to him under that disguise. In that case, there was at least a fair chance that he might also be known to Sir Wilfred's associates. To some member of his family, or to the staff at his office. Arnold made a note to inquire upon this point. Then he realised that all this was based upon the supposition that the pistol had belonged to Sir Wilfred.

Well, everything tended to support that assumption, with the exception of a single detail. The firearms experts had reported that the pistol had seen some service. It had fired several rounds, and been carefully looked after by its owner. Sir Wilfred had at one time been fond of target practice. He might have amused himself with the pistol, and could have been trusted to look after it. But when and where had he used it? In Shrubb Court? Impossible. Then at home? Then, surely, his niece would have known something about it. And to complicate the problem, an old question cropped up again. If Sir Wilfred had bought the pistol as a means of committing suicide, it was understandable that he should not have taken out a certificate for it. But would a magistrate, the Chairman of the local Bench, infringe the law in the case of a weapon used for perfectly legitimate purposes?

It seemed to Arnold that the pistol, instead of furnishing a valuable clue, as he had hoped, was merely an additional complication. He realised that, in spite of his discoveries in connection with the tunnel, he was as far as ever from being able to prove that Sir Wilfred had been murdered. The theory of suicide was not even disproved. He knew well enough what the assistant commissioner would say, when he made his report. However, realising that the report must be made, Arnold went to see his chief.

Sir Edric Conway, the Assistant Commissioner, who, incidentally was a personal friend of Merrion's, listened to Arnold with close attention. "It's a very queer story," he said. "The obvious thing is that these men, whom you call A and B, held up the train in order to give A the chance of murdering Saxonby and getting away with it. But I needn't point out to you that, obvious as it is, there is no proved connection between the two men and Saxonby's death. Even if we knew who they were, we should have no direct evidence against them. The pistol, you say, doesn't help you. You're quite certain that it is the weapon with which Saxonby was killed?"

No doubts upon this point had occurred to Arnold. "Well, sir, since it was found in the compartment, with one cartridge fired, one can only assume so," he replied.

"Assumption is no good. You've got to be in a position to prove it. How do you know that Saxonby was not killed with a similar pistol, carried by the murderer? You say that there is a possibility that Saxonby had this particular weapon in his pocket. Very well.

The murderer, after shooting him with his own gun, found this one in his pocket, fired a single shot from it, and then threw it on the floor of the compartment. I don't say that's what actually happened, mind. I'm only thinking of the lines the defence may take if we're ever lucky enough to lay hands on our man."

"The only way to prove that this pistol is the one with which Sir Wilfred was killed, sir, is to find the bullet. The men from the carriage department of the railway company are taking out the upholstery of the compartment to-day, under Inspector Marden's supervision."

"I was going to suggest that, but I see you've thought of it already. Very well, go ahead, and stick to the job till you find out something definite."

Following his interview with the assistant commissioner, Arnold paid a visit to Shrubb Court, where he asked for Mr. Torrance. The secretary saw him at once. "I'm always at your disposal, Mr. Arnold," he said. "If there's anything I can do for you, you've only got to let me know."

"Thanks, I shan't keep you long," Arnold replied. "I only want to ask a few questions. To begin with, do you think it possible that on Thursday last Sir Wilfred was taking home anything of value from here?"

"Nothing in any way connected with the firm, certainly. Anything of any value is kept in this room, in that safe you can see in the corner. Sir Wilfred didn't keep a key of the safe, since of recent years he has never had occasion to use it. There are only two keys in existence. Richard Saxonby has one, and I have the other."

"Where were those keys last Thursday, Mr. Torrance?"

"One of them is at the bank, where Mr. Richard deposited it before he went to America. The other I gave to my assistant on Tuesday evening so that he could open the safe while I was in Manchester. He gave it back to me on Friday morning. As usual, it was only opened twice a day, to take out the petty cash and so forth in the morning, and replace it in the evening. And I can assure you that nothing else was taken out of it in my absence."

"Six Wilfred might have received something of a private nature during the day?"

Torrance smiled. "I wasn't here, you know," he replied. "I suppose he might have, but I can't imagine what it could have been."

"Did you go to Manchester as a matter of ordinary routine?" Arnold asked.

"Well, yes and no. I go there at intervals, but I should not have gone there last week under ordinary circumstances. With both Mr. Richard and Mrs. Wardour away, I am more or less in charge here. But, when he was up here the week before, Sir Wilfred seemed a little uneasy about the new manager we have at our Manchester office. He said he'd like me to go up for a couple of days, and see how he was getting on. And we decided that Wednesday and Thursday would be the best."

Arnold made no comment upon this. "There is reason to believe that Sir Wilfred had a friend, or at all events an acquaintance, whom I am anxious to trace," he said. "He is an elderly man, probably between sixty and seventy. He appears to be somewhat infirm, stoops, and walks with difficulty. He wears a short grey beard. Does that description convey anybody to you?"

"Well, I don't know," replied Torrance doubtfully. "It's a bit vague, isn't it? But it might apply to old Mr. Dredger, who used to be our manager in Manchester, and retired early this year. He is sixty-five, and wears a short grey beard. But he was hardly infirm when I last saw him. However, he has been ill since then, and that may account for it."

"Can you give me Mr. Dredger's address?"

"Certainly. He lives with his widowed daughter-in-law at 75 London Road, Blackdown."

It cost Arnold a considerable effort to conceal his amazement at this information. He buried himself in making a note of this address, then changed the subject. "You told me that Sir Wilfred had a visitor on Thursday afternoon," he said. "A man who gave the name of Yates. You know nothing of him, I think you said?"

"Nothing whatever. And nobody else in the office seems to have seen him before. Somebody who knew Sir Wilfred at Mavis Court, I expect."

"I wonder if I could have a description of him?"

"Nothing easier. I'll send for the clerk who interviewed him."

The clerk, upon being questioned, remembered Mr. Yates perfectly. A very pleasant-spoken gentleman, somewhere between twenty and thirty. Tall, dark, clean-shaven, exceptionally well-dressed. Was carrying nothing but a pair of gloves and an umbrella. Since he had an appointment, was not asked his business. Sir Wilfred was evidently expecting him, for as soon as he was announced, he had ordered him to be sent to his room at once. Mr. Yates had not stayed more than a few minutes.

"I can't offer any suggestion," said Torrance, when the clerk had gone. "Now and then Sir Wilfred had personal visitors when he was here, but they were usually old business friends who dropped in to see him, and of course I knew them all. This Mr. Yates is a new one on me."

"Well, I mustn't take up too much of your time. Just one more question. Do you keep a record of the numbers of five-pound notes that pass through the office?"

"I expect so. But it's hardly my department. Come along and see the cashier."

Arnold repeated his question to the cashier, who replied in the affirmative. The inspector gave him a slip of paper, on which were written the number of the notes found in the wallet. "Have you any record of these?" he asked.

The cashier compared the slip of paper with his book. "Yes, I have," he replied. "They are among a number of notes drawn by me from the bank last Monday, a week ago to-day."

This was more than Arnold had dared to hope for. "And can you tell me how you disposed of them?" he asked.

"Certainly. They are booked out to Sir Wilfred. On Thursday morning he sent me down a private cheque to be cashed, for twenty pounds, asking for three five-pound notes and five one-pound notes. These are the numbers of the notes which I gave him."

Arnold next produced the wallet, now emptied of its contents. "Do you recognise that, Mr. Torrance?" he asked.

Torrance took the wallet, opened it, closed it again, and returned it to the inspector. "Sir Wilfred's," he said briefly.

"Can you be absolutely certain of that?" Arnold asked. "You have never actually handled the wallet before, I suppose?"

Torrance smiled. "I've never handled it, certainly," he replied, "but I've seen Sir Wilfred take it out of his pocket, often enough. I suppose, if you were to put me in the witness-box, I couldn't actually swear that this was the one. But I haven't the slightest doubt that it is."

Arnold was about to leave the office, when a remark from Torrance detained him. "By the way, Mrs. Wardour looked in here this morning," he said. "She's just back from the South of France. She's gone down to Mavis Court. The funeral was this afternoon, you know."

"Did her husband come back with her?" Arnold asked.

"Well, no. She told me that her husband came back to England some days ago, leaving her out there. I gather that Sir Wilfred's scheme for effecting a reconciliation between them was not altogether successful. She told me that she had not seen her husband since her return."

"Where do the Wardours live?"

"They've got a house in Hampstead, and a cottage near Saffron Walden in Essex. Latterly, since the disagreement between them, Mrs. Wardour has spent most of her time in Hampstead, and Major Wardour in the country."

Arnold made a note of the two addresses, and returned to Scotland Yard.

XI

THE INSPECTOR'S INQUIRIES AT THE OFFICES OF MESSRS. Wigland and Bunthorne had considerably shaken his faith in Merrion's theory. Certainly, Merrion's conjecture that Torrance's visit to Manchester had been at Sir Wilfred's instigation had proved correct. But for the rest the evidence was against him.

His theory had been founded upon an imaginary substitution of the wallets. But it seemed to Arnold very doubtful that any such substitution had taken place. Torrance was certain that the wallet found in the dead man's pocket had been the property of Sir Wilfred. Miss Olivia, on the other hand, was positive that this was not the case. Miss Olivia, it might be argued, should know best. She had actually handled and repaired the wallet, while Torrance admitted that he had never handled it.

But the evidence of the notes was entirely in Torrance's favour. The notes found in the wallet were demonstrably those given to Sir Wilfred by his cashier on Thursday morning. Now, according to Merrion's theory, the wallets had been interchanged for one definite reason, to save the time which must otherwise have been expended in extracting object X from Sir Wilfred's wallet, and then replacing this in his pocket. But, since the notes were in Sir Wilfred's wallet, which Merrion had called number one, if an exchange had been made, they must have been transferred to number two. What, then, had been gained, either in time or convenience? It would have been as easy to remove object X from Sir Wilfred's wallet as to transfer the notes.

Again, what proof was there of the existence of this mysterious object? None whatever. Perhaps the man who had given his name as

Yates had handed it to Sir Wilfred during their interview. But that he had done so was a matter of pure conjecture.

Finally, there was the wholly unexpected emergence of Mr. Dredger, who lived at Blackdown. Arnold fully realised that, pending identification, Mr. Dredger must not be taken too seriously. Elderly men with short grey beards were not uncommon. Torrance had recognised him from a very sketchy second-hand description. He might have been entirely mistaken. Still, it was remarkable that Mr. Dredger lived at Blackdown, of all places in the world. He would have to be interviewed, of that there could be no doubt.

Merrion had advised Arnold not to lose sight of Major Wardour. Here, again, was a disturbing factor. Wardour was said to have returned to England some days ago. How long ago? Before November 14th, the day on which Sir Wilfred had been killed? What had he to gain by the death of his father-in-law?

Arnold decided that it was too late to pursue his inquiries that evening. But early next morning he went once more to Blackdown, and made his way to 75 London Road. He found this to be a substantial and well-kept villa, and upon ringing the bell he found that Mr. Dredger was at home. He was taken to a comfortably-furnished sitting-room, where an elderly man was reading a newspaper in front of a bright fire. He looked up as Arnold was announced. The inspector's first impression was of a short grey beard, then of a lined and wrinkled face and a hook nose. In a flash he remembered Miss Clutsam's description. Like a parrot, she had said.

Mr. Dredger certainly seemed surprised to see his visitor. But his manners were beyond reproach. "Sit down here by the fire, inspector," he said. "It's cold out, I've no doubt. That's right. Now, what can I have the pleasure of doing for you?"

"You can give me some information, if you will, Mr. Dredger," Arnold replied. "To begin with, I want you to fix your mind upon last Thursday. The date was November 14th."

"I'm not likely to forget it. That was the day Sir Wilfred shot himself. And whatever he did it for passes my comprehension. A man in his position, without a care in the world! It must have been Lady Saxonby's death, preying on his mind, though he never showed it. And there's another reason why I shouldn't forget last Thursday. It was the day my daughter—at least, she's not my daughter, but my dead son's wife, but I always call her my daughter—was called down to Plymouth on a fool's errand."

"I see you remember the day well enough. Can you tell me how you employed your time?"

"No difficulty about that. It was about nine o'clock, when we were having breakfast, that the telegram came. My daughter was terribly upset, for the lad is her only nephew, the son of her brother that's dead, and she's always been very fond of him. So she went off at once…"

"One moment, Mr. Dredger," Arnold interposed. "You're going a bit too fast for me. Who is this lad, and what was the telegram about?"

"Harold, his name is. He's been working this last couple of years in a house-agent's office at Plymouth. And very well he's doing, from all accounts. Well, on Thursday morning, Alice, that's my daughter, you understand, got this telegram. It said that Harold had met with a serious accident, and asked her to come down at once. The telegram was signed Fred, which is the name of Harold's chum in the office.

"Well, as I say, the poor girl was terribly upset, and went off at once. She caught the 10.30 at Paddington, and when she got to Plymouth went straight to the office to make inquiries. And the first person she saw was Harold, fit as a fiddle, and nothing whatever wrong with him. He'd never had an accident, and the whole thing was a hoax. They tackled Fred, and he swore he'd never sent the wire. However, Alice stayed down there that night, and they had a very good time between them, from what I can make out. I shouldn't wonder if those two young fellows hadn't fixed it up between them, to get Alice down there."

"So that you were left alone for the whole of Thursday, Mr. Dredger?"

"And the best part of Friday, too. Alice didn't get back until late that afternoon."

"Rather hard on you, wasn't it? How did you get on?"

"Oh, I can manage to take care of myself, as a rule. In the morning I went out for a run in my car, as I pretty well always do. You see, I'm not so young as I was, and walking bothers me. But the doctor says that it's good for me to get out for a bit every day, even if it's only in a car."

"Do you remember where you went?"

"Why, yes. I went to Medbridge, had a look in at the market, and came home again. I was back here for lunch at one o'clock."

"Did you see anybody you knew at Medbridge?"

"I can't say that I did. But then I don't know many people that way."

"Did you have any trouble with the car?" Arnold asked.

Mr. Dredger looked at him shrewdly. "Oh, so that's it, is it?" he replied. "I've been wondering all this time what you've been after. There's been an accident, I suppose, and you think I was involved. No. I had no trouble with the car of any kind, and I neither saw nor heard of any accident. You can see the car for yourself, if you like. She's shabby, but you won't find that she's been damaged."

"I'd like to see the car later. Now, what did you do after lunch? It was a nice bright day, I remember. You went out again, didn't you?"

Mr. Dredger shook his head. "I couldn't do that, with Alice away," he replied. "You see, it was the maid's afternoon out, and somebody has to stay at home and look after the house. I never set foot out of doors again after lunch. The maid went out about half-past two and came back at ten. I made myself a cup of tea, and cooked myself a bit of supper, and as soon as the maid had come in I went to bed."

"Did you have any visitors during the afternoon or evening?"

"No, I didn't see a soul. I spent the best part of my time reading. I'm very fond of a good book, and since I've retired I read a lot."

"Do you ever go up to London, Mr. Dredger?"

"Now and again. I drop in sometimes to see my friends at Wigland and Bunthorne's. Torrance, the secretary, is a very decent chap, and Mr. Richard—Sir Richard, he'll be now, I suppose, was always glad to see me. But I've not been up for several weeks now. I had a touch of arthritis, and it's made it a bit difficult for me to get about."

"It didn't occur to you, since you were alone, to go up on Thursday?"

"I never gave it a thought. I wouldn't have gone out and left the house empty. I haven't a word to say against the police, inspector, but places do get burgled sometimes."

"Yes, I'm afraid they do. Did you think of going out in your car this morning, Mr. Dredger?"

"Why, yes. It's a bit cold, but I don't mind that if it's fine. I shall take a short run directly, I dare say."

"I wonder if you would take me with you? I want to go to a farm not far from Little Hazelbury. Do you know that road?"

Mr. Dredger showed no discomfort at the mention of this village. "I'll take you, willingly enough, inspector," he replied. "I know the way to Little Hazelbury well enough. Turn off to the right from the main Medbridge road, and then again to the left. I don't often go that way, for it's very narrow and winding. But we'll find the place, right enough."

Mr. Dredger's car was garaged in a shed at the end of his garden, the doors of which opened on to a back street. Arnold noticed that the comings and goings of the car could not be overlooked from the house. The car itself was a miniature saloon, of respectable age but apparently in good condition. They took their places in it, Mr. Dredger at the wheel, and set off.

The drive was uneventful. Mr. Dredger's driving, though by no means spectacular, was sufficiently cautious to satisfy the most exacting. They followed the same route as Arnold and Merrion had taken on the previous morning. The inspector was on the look-out, and when they reached the lane which led past the shaft, he spoke. "The farm I want to get to lies along there," he said. "Have you ever been down this lane before, Mr. Dredger?"

"Never," replied Mr. Dredger, as he obediently turned the car in the required direction. "But there's no harm in trying, I suppose."

Arnold made no further remark until they came in sight of the tunnel ventilating shaft. "What's that thing like a short chimney, smoking away over there?" he asked casually.

"Couldn't say," replied Mr. Dredger briefly. "I've never seen it before."

Shortly afterwards Arnold caught sight of the farmer, walking along the lane towards them. "Why, there's the very man I want to speak to!" he exclaimed. "Would you mind pulling up when we reach him?"

Mr. Dredger nodded. They went on for a short distance, then, as the car stopped, Arnold slipped quietly out of it. The farmer stared at the car, then at Mr. Dredger. "Back again, then?" he asked pleasantly.

"Back again?" replied Mr. Dredger. "What do you mean?"

"Why, just what I say. I'm the chap what helped you push the car on to the grass over by the stack yonder, that day when it broke down last week. Don't you remember me?"

"I never remember setting eyes on you before," replied Mr. Dredger indignantly. "My car never broke down last week, here or anywhere else. You're mistaking me for somebody else."

The farmer winked knowingly. "You can't kid me," he said. "I knew you the moment I set eyes on you, aye, and the car too."

Arnold, who had remained in the background, now came forward. "You say you've seen this gentleman before?" he asked innocently.

The farmer began to imagine that he was being made the object of some obscure joke. "Yes, and I've seen you before," he replied tartly. "You and another gentleman spoke to me about this very time yesterday. And it's no good your saying that you didn't, for I know better."

"I shouldn't venture to say anything of the kind," said Arnold hastily. "But you hear what this gentleman says. Are you sure you aren't mistaken about him?"

"Not I. I know him, right enough. He's the bloke I told you about yesterday. He drove along in this very car, and then stopped. He told me the car had broken down, and I helped him push it out of the road."

"That's ridiculous!" exclaimed Mr. Dredger. "When do you say this happened?"

"Last Thursday, round about noon, as you know as well as I do."

"Quite a number of unusual things seem to have happened last Thursday, Mr. Dredger," said Arnold quietly. Then, turning to the farmer, "You're sure it was the same car?"

"I wouldn't go so far as to swear, not knowing much about cars myself. But, if it wasn't this very car, it was the very spit of it."

"This seems most extraordinary," said Arnold. "Would you mind turning the car, Mr. Dredger, and driving back to where this man says he helped you to push the car on to the grass?"

Mr. Dredger seemed too bewildered to make any objection. Arnold and the farmer walked to the shaft, with the car following behind them. "That's the place," said the farmer. "You can see the tracks of the car still. Aye, and the tracks of the lorry what came to draw it away."

The tracks were certainly there, though no longer very distinct. Enough of them, however, could be discerned to show that they had been made by a set of Dunlop tyres, with the treads in good condition. Arnold looked significantly at Mr. Dredger's car, which was equipped with a set of nearly new Dunlops. "Are you quite sure you didn't lose your way last Thursday, Mr. Dredger?" he asked.

The farmer interposed, before Mr. Dredger could reply. "That's just what it was. He'd lost his way. Told me he wanted to get to Little Hazelbury. And I told him he ought to have kept on, instead of turning down here like he'd done." He turned upon Mr. Dredger, almost belligerently. "You're never going to deny that, now, when you know it's the gospel truth?"

Mr. Dredger became purple in the face. "Of course I deny it!" he exclaimed.

"Then I say you're a blinking liar," replied the farmer. "Likely enough you were up to no good, and you don't want this gentleman to know it. Well, it's your affair and not mine. But, mark my word, you'll come to no good. And you with one foot in the grave, so to say." And with this the farmer departed about his business, surrounded by an aura of virtuous indignation.

Arnold let him go, and said nothing until he was well out of earshot. Then he remarked lightly, "We all suffer at times from a defective memory, Mr. Dredger. Won't you think again about what you did last Thursday? Let me try to help you. You went out for your usual morning drive. But you didn't go all the way to Medbridge. You turned off the road, and came here instead. Then, with our friend's assistance, you pushed the car on to the grass beside the shaft. Then you walked back to the main road and, I dare say, took a bus home. About half-past five that evening, a breakdown lorry came and took the car away. Don't you remember, now?"

Mr. Dredger passed his hand across his forehead. "I don't understand it," he replied pathetically. "I'm no longer a young man, but my memory is perfectly good. I'm ready to swear that what I have already told you about my doings last Thursday is perfectly true."

"And yet, curiously enough, you can't call any witnesses to support you?"

"That's not my fault. As it happened, after my daughter left, I spoke to nobody all day, except to the maid at lunch-time, and when she came home in the evening."

"It is unfortunate that you have no witnesses, Mr. Dredger, for there are quite a number on my side. The farmer who has just left us, for one. And two ladies, whom I'm sure you'll enjoy meeting again." The inspector's voice hardened suddenly. "Now, hadn't you better make a clean breast of it?"

"I have told you the truth, and I shall adhere to it," replied Mr. Dredger, not without dignity.

"Then there is nothing for it but to ask you to drive me back to Blackdown. And, if you will be so good, we will stop at the police-station."

Even this remark, intentionally ominous, did not shake Mr. Dredger. They drove back in grim silence, and the car pulled up at the police-station. Arnold got out. "I need not trouble you any further, Mr. Dredger," he said. "I should go home now, if I were you, and think things over a bit. We shall meet again very shortly, I haven't a doubt." And he walked into the building.

Here he had a conversation with the local inspector, who was acquainted with Mr. Dredger. Arnold told him as much of the story as he thought fit, and succeeded in exciting his colleague's surprise. Dredger had the reputation of being a quiet old stick, and was the last man in the world whom one would suspect of engaging in a desperate enterprise. Mrs. Dredger, his daughter-in-law, had lived in the town for a long time, and was highly respected. However, if Mr. Arnold liked, inquiries should be made locally for anybody who might have seen Mr. Dredger on the previous Thursday. And, in addition, a watch should be kept on his future movements. Assured of this, Arnold returned to Scotland Yard, with yet another puzzle to be disentangled.

That Mr. Dredger was the murderer, he did not for a moment believe. It was incredible that a man of his age and infirmities should have performed a feat which demanded the highest degree of agility. But it was not impossible that Sir Wilfred had been the victim of a conspiracy, and that the late manager of his Manchester office was one of the conspirators. If so, what was the exact significance of the part which he had played?

The telegram which had called Mrs. Dredger from home was deeply suspicious. Had such a telegram really been sent? That was easily discovered. Arnold wrote a note to the Plymouth police, asking them to search the files of the various telegraph offices in the borough. In any case, his daughter-in-law's absence had resulted in Mr. Dredger being alone, and unquestioned, that Thursday. It was doubly convenient that it should have been the maid's day out. Mr. Dredger could come and go unobserved. His own account of his actions could not be contradicted. And a very unsatisfactory account it was.

He had declared that he had driven to Medbridge. That was natural, for, to reach the tunnel shaft, he would have to leave Blackdown by the Medbridge road. Any of his acquaintances might have seen him doing so, and recognised him. But had he actually got as far as

Medbridge? He might even have done that, and turned off to the shaft on his way back.

Then came the matter of the farmer's instant recognition of him. The farmer's statement was above suspicion. What possible reason could he have for spinning a false yarn? Besides, his manner had carried complete conviction. There could be no doubt that he firmly believed that the man whom he had seen on Thursday, and Mr. Dredger, were one and the same. Further, the independent evidence of the tyre marks was not to be lost sight of. A very large percentage of cars were fitted with Dunlop tyres, certainly. Mr. Dredger's car was of the mass-production type, turned out by the thousand, and the farmer could not be expected to swear to the individual vehicle. Yet all these details helped to swing the balance against Mr. Dredger. And in the other scale was nothing but his own unsupported statement.

On the whole, it seemed highly probable that Mr. Dredger had driven his car to the shaft on Thursday morning, and left it there. If he had done so, it could only have been as a pretext for the visit of the breakdown lorry in the evening. The lorry, with its equipment, had been essential to the drama in the tunnel. Then it followed that Mr. Dredger had connived at the performance of that drama, and thus at the murder of Sir Wilfred.

Had his part in the conspiracy ended there? Or had he actually travelled up to London in the afternoon, and come back by the five o'clock train from Cannon Street? He must be confronted with the Clutsam ladies. That was obviously the next step. If they recognised him, what then? There was a link missing somewhere. By a stretch of the imagination Arnold could contemplate the possibility that he had shot Sir Wilfred, who would not have been unduly alarmed at seeing his old manager enter his compartment. What the inspector could not contemplate was Mr. Dredger leaping from the moving train, and being hauled out of the darkness of the tunnel with a rope.

But Arnold felt that he could afford to leave Mr. Dredger to enjoy his freedom. It was not at all unlikely that he would attempt to communicate with his fellow-conspirators, or they with him. Meanwhile, there were other matters to be attended to. First and foremost, a small package from Inspector Marden.

XII

AFTER UNWRAPPING MANY SHEETS OF PAPER, ARNOLD REACHED the kernel of the packet, which proved to be a misshapen pellet of lead. Accompanying it was a note from Marden. "The enclosed was found behind the upholstery of the railway compartment in which Sir Wilfred Saxonby's body was found. As you will see, though badly flattened, it is still recognisable as a bullet. There is a faint mark on the steel partition, where the bullet struck it. The position of this mark corresponds with that of the wound, supposing Sir Wilfred to have been sitting upright at the time he was shot. It also corresponds with the hole in the upholstery, seen by you."

Arnold wasted no time over the bullet, but sent it straight to the firearms experts, for comparison with the pistol. This done, he turned his attention to the arrears of work, unconnected with the present case, which awaited him. This occupied him for the rest of the afternoon.

Next morning he took a train to Saffron Walden. His first call was at the police station, where he inquired what was known about the Wardours. Of Mrs. Wardour, he found, very little was known. She was not often in the neighbourhood, and it was understood that she spent most of her time in London. Major Wardour, however, was a familiar figure. He lived some little distance outside the town, where he owned a small house, to which was attached a fair-sized poultry farm. He had been abroad recently, but had now returned.

"What sort of a fellow is he?" Arnold asked.

"Oh, he's all right, if you take him the proper way," was the reply. "His temper is a bit uncertain, and he has quarrelled with a good many people round here. But he can be pleasant enough when he chooses."

"Am I likely to find him at home if I go over to his place now?"

"Certain to. He's always at home in the morning, messing around his fowl-houses. He's quite a successful poultry farmer, they say."

Arnold, having ascertained the way to get to Major Wardour's house, set out on foot, and covered the distance in half an hour or so. He rang the bell, and after some delay the door was answered by a forbidding-looking woman, with a scrubbing-brush in her hand. No, the major was not in. He'd be about the farm somewhere. And Arnold found the door slammed in his face.

Nothing daunted, he walked round to the back of the house and looked about him. Some little distance away he saw a masculine figure moving about among a group of chicken-houses. He walked towards him, and was within a few yards of the man before his approach was noticed. The man was tall and muscular, with a heavy, not over intelligent expression, and dressed in breeches and a shooting coat. He eyed Arnold suspiciously. "Who are you, and what do you want?" he asked gruffly.

"I am Inspector Arnold, from Scotland Yard. You are Major Wardour, I believe?"

"Your belief is correct," replied the other. "I thought perhaps you were an official of the Egg Marketing Board. They're always coming here and worrying me about something or other. Well, what can I do for you?"

Arnold smiled disarmingly. "You can answer a few questions, if you will. In the first place, what is your Christian name, Major Wardour? I want to be certain that I'm talking to the right person."

"Stephen. Major Stephen Wardour, retired. Late of the Royal Rutlandshires. Now trying to make a living by persuading a lot of damn obstinate fowls to lay eggs. How does that suit you?"

"Perfectly," Arnold replied. And he meant it. Merrion's wild guess had come off. The man's initials actually were S. W. But it had got to be shown whether there was any significance in that. "You've been abroad lately, haven't you, Major Wardour?" Arnold continued.

"And if I have, is it any affair of yours?" Wardour replied. "Don't think I want to be rude, but I think I have a right to know your reasons for questioning me."

It was clear to Arnold that Wardour was a person who must be treated with considerable tact. "I am engaged in investigating the death of Sir Wilfred Saxonby," he replied simply.

"My late lamented father-in-law? So that's it, is it! I saw by the papers that the inquest had been adjourned. There's no doubt that he shot himself, is there?"

Arnold parried the question. "Can you suggest any reason why he should have shot himself, Major Wardour?"

Wardour shrugged his shoulders. "When a fellow does away with himself, it is usually for some reason that he doesn't care to talk about," he replied. "I'm afraid that I was never sufficiently in Saxonby's confidence to know much about his private affairs. Have you spoken to my wife?"

"Not yet," said the inspector. "I wanted to talk to you first."

Wardour grinned. "Just as well, perhaps. Irene and I are rather at loggerheads just now, and she might have painted me in darker colours than I deserve. Well, go ahead, but I warn you in advance that I can't throw the faintest glimmer of light on Saxonby's death."

"Well, to begin with, you and Mrs. Wardour were abroad together, weren't you? Was it your suggestion or hers?"

"Neither. It was Saxonby's. He suddenly felt called upon to adopt the role of peacemaker. It's no good making any secret of the fact that Irene and I don't get on together. We haven't for years. I dare say it's my own fault, but I can't stand being nagged at. And I'm inclined to get a bit short tempered when Irene tries it on. So she spends most of her time at the house in Hampstead, which, by the way, is hers, and I spend most of mine here. This place, also by the way, belongs to me.

"Saxonby was well aware of this, and it never seemed to worry him. My brother-in-law, Richard, who, between ourselves, is a bit of a prig, tried to lecture me on the subject once, but I soon put him in his place. And then, last month, Saxonby asked me to meet him at his office on an urgent matter. I went, and, bless me, if he didn't begin to talk about Irene! I was never so surprised in my life."

"Would it be impertinent to ask what he said?"

"Not a bit. He said that it grieved him to see Irene and me living apart, and that he was very anxious to do something to draw us together again. Of course, I put my ears up at that. I asked him straight out if Irene or Richard had been getting at him. He told me positively that they had not, and he wasn't a man to tell a deliberate lie without some very good reason for it."

"Had he any proposition to put forward?" Arnold asked.

"Rather! He suggested that we should take Irene's car and go for a motoring trip in the south of France. He said that if we were both interested and amused, and away from our usual haunts, we should probably be able to hit it off together. I had my doubts, and told him that I didn't think it would do much good. But he insisted, and begged me to try the experiment, as a personal favour to him. If it failed, things would be no worse than before. So at last, seeing that he was absolutely set upon it, I agreed.

"And then, to my astonishment, I found that he had everything cut and dried. We were to go on the seventh of this month, and stay at least a fortnight. He said that I mustn't say anything to Irene, for he would talk to her, and he knew that she would consent. I wasn't a bit keen on the idea, and I tried to think of objections. The only one that occurred to me was rather feeble, I'm afraid. There are only two directors of Wigland and Bunthorne, Irene and Richard. Richard had just gone to America, and, though I don't suppose that Irene is much of a business asset to the firm, this would mean that both directors were away together. However, Saxonby swept all that aside. Torrance, the secretary, was quite capable of looking after things. And Saxonby himself would come up to London if anything out of the way happened.

"Well, to make a long story short, we went. Fortunately, I've got a chap here who can be trusted to look after things in my absence. We took the car over and started to drive across France. Irene seemed to enjoy it, but I was bored stiff. And we didn't seem to hit it off any better than usual. Where Irene wanted to go, I didn't, and what I wanted to do, she didn't. You know how it is when two people are like that, I dare say. I stuck it as long as I could, and then I chucked my hand in. I left Irene with the car to go her own way and came home by train and boat."

"When did you come home, Major Wardour?"

"I left Irene at Cannes on Wednesday, the 13th, and got to London next day, at about half-past three."

That was on the very day of Sir Wilfred's death! It seemed to Arnold that in whatever direction he pursued his inquiries, that particular date gained some new significance. But he allowed nothing of his thoughts to escape him. "You got back to London about half-past three on Thursday," he said. "What did you do then?"

"Oh, just mooched about. Called at the club, looked in at Leadenhall Market, went to a shop or two. Nothing particular. Stood myself a bite of dinner, and came down here afterwards. And here I've been ever since."

"You didn't go to Sir Wilfred's funeral yesterday?"

"No. Sent a wreath instead. Guessed that Irene would have heard the news and hurried back. I'm not particularly anxious to meet her. We had words when we parted."

"Do you know any of the staff of Wigland and Bunthorne, Major Wardour?"

"Any of the chaps in the office, you mean? Oh, yes, I know most of them slightly. Irene has introduced me. Torrance is the best of them. Very capable fellow. Saxonby always looked on him as his right hand, and told him more than he ever told anybody else, even Irene or Richard. If he can't tell you why Saxonby shot himself, then you may take it from me that nobody else can."

"In the course of Thursday afternoon Sir Wilfred had a visitor who seems to have been a complete stranger to the staff. He gave his name as Yates. Do you know of any such person?"

"Yates? That's the name of Saxonby's lawyer. Not the one who looks after the legal business of the firm, but his private solicitor. A man of about Saxonby's own age, with a thin face and a sarcastic way of talking."

"I'm afraid that description will hardly fit," Arnold remarked. "This man is described as young and smartly dressed."

"Well, old Yates has a son, whom he has just admitted to partnership. Bit of a lad, I believe, though I've never met him. He may be your man. His office is in Coleman Street, if you want to know. I forget the number."

"Thank you, Major Wardour," Arnold replied. "I'll make a note of that. By the way, are you interested in shooting?"

"Game shooting, you mean? I do a bit now and then, but not very often. I have quite enough birds to kill without that. I've been out once or twice with Saxonby at Mavis Court. He was a very fine shot in his day. I've no doubt that's why he chose a pistol to finish himself off with. Knew he'd make a clean job of it."

"As a soldier, I expect you are a good shot with a pistol?"

"Pretty fair. Better than I am with a scattergun anyhow. This place is infested with rats. They come after the chicken food, you know. I go after them sometimes with a little automatic I've got, and I usually account for a good few of them. It's not bad sport."

"I dare say it is very good fun. What sort of automatic have you?"

"Oh, just a cheap little thing, .22 calibre, which I happened to see in a shop in Brussels when I was over there at the beginning of the year. I've taken out a certificate for it, so you needn't suspect me of infringing the law."

"I wonder if I might see the pistol and the certificate, Major Wardour?"

"I don't see why you shouldn't. But you'll have to come back to the house. I don't carry it about with me, you know."

They returned to the house, which now appeared to be empty. Wardour led the way into a sitting-room, in which was a massive oak desk, littered with papers. He pulled open one of the drawers and looked into it with an expression of astonishment. "Hallo!" he exclaimed. "Where's it gone to? That's very queer."

"Is the pistol not in its usual place?" Arnold asked casually.

"No, it isn't. And there's a box of ammunition missing. I had two boxes of a hundred each. One I had opened and taken a few rounds from. That's gone. The other unopened one is still here."

"Perhaps you put the pistol and the missing box in some other drawer by mistake," Arnold suggested.

"I'm pretty sure I didn't. Somebody must have moved them. But they can't be far off."

Wardour set to work to ransack the desk, turning everything on to the floor. But his search was unsuccessful. "Well, that beats me!" he exclaimed. "Where the dickens can the blessed things have got to?"

"When did you last see the pistol?" Arnold asked.

"Now I come to think of it, I haven't seen it since I came back from France. I have had no occasion to use it, so I haven't opened this drawer until now. But I had the pistol out the day before I went away, and shot half a dozen rats with it. And I distinctly remember cleaning it and putting it away in its usual place."

"That was on Wednesday, the 6th. Do you think that any of the servants are likely to have interfered with it?"

Wardour laughed. "I don't keep a staff of servants. Only Mrs. Grader, who lives in a cottage down the road, and comes in and out as seems good to her. She wouldn't have touched it. Then there's the chap I employ on the farm, but he never comes inside the house."

"Was the house shut up while you were away?"

"Oh, no. Mrs. Grader came and went as usual, or so I believe. She took advantage of my absence to have what she calls a thorough turn-out."

"Does she lock the doors and windows when she is not here?"

"Only at night. There's nothing of any value about the place, and I've never had anything taken. My chap is always about, and people know that, I expect."

"Still, it is not impossible that somebody entered the house during your absence, opened the drawer, and took the pistol?"

"I suppose it's possible. But why should they take the pistol and a few cartridges, and leave everything else? There's nothing else missing, so far as I'm aware."

"They may have had some particular reason for doing so," said Arnold significantly. "Is there any way in which the pistol could be identified?"

"It would be identified by the maker's number, which you'll see on the certificate. That's still here. And there's another thing. When I bought the pistol the chap in the shop told me I could have my initials put on it free of charge. So I told him to engrave my initials, S.W., in a monogram. And quite a neat job he made of it."

"Then the pistol should not be difficult to trace. Now, can you tell me who knew that you possessed it?"

"Oh, pretty well everybody. Lots of people have seen me use it. My chap, of course, and, I suppose, Mrs. Grader. Saxonby knew, for one day when he was here he tried his hand at it, and a pretty good show he made. Irene knows, of course. Richard, because he's seen me use it. Any one who has been here this year, in fact."

"Have any of the staff of Wigland and Bunthorne ever been here?"

"None of the London staff. A funny old chap called Dredger, who used to run the Manchester office, came and spent the day here a few months ago."

Was this a fresh link in the chain, Arnold wondered. "Is this Mr. Dredger a personal friend of yours?" he asked idly.

"Oh, dear, no. I'd never met him before. It was Irene who told me about him. It seems that when he retired he thought of taking up poultry keeping, and Irene asked me if I would mind having him down here and putting him up to dodges. So he came along, and seemed quite a decent old chap. But when he saw that there was quite a lot of hard work involved, he gave up the idea. I haven't seen him since."

"Did Mr. Dredger see the pistol while he was here?"

"Yes, he did. I was telling him that rats were always a nuisance, and he asked me what I did about it. So I took out the pistol and showed it to him."

Arnold had now learnt as much as he wanted to know for the present. Having secured the remaining box of ammunition, on the pretext that it might assist in the recovery of the pistol, he returned to Scotland Yard.

The firearms experts had completed their examination of the flattened bullet. "We can say definitely that it was fired from the pistol already examined," they reported. "Enough of the marks of the rifling remains to establish that fact. There happens to be a slight irregularity in one of the grooves of the pistol, and that irregularity is reproduced on the bullet."

This was satisfactory. The maker's number on the pistol corresponded with that on Wardour's certificate. And, upon being shown the box of ammunition, the experts declared its contents to be exactly similar to those of the other two samples which they had examined.

Arnold sat down to digest the information he had acquired. But, before doing so, he wrote a note to Merrion. He felt that his friend's powers of imagination would assist him in the sorting out of this queer jumble of facts. Then he took pencil and paper and made a few notes of what seemed to him most significant.

"Sir Wilfred was shot with the pistol found in the compartment. This is proved by the identification of the bullet.

"This pistol belonged to Major Wardour. Proved by the maker's number and the initials engraved upon it.

"The pistol was in Major Wardour's possession as recently as November 6th, eight days before Sir Wilfred's death. Wardour was in London during the afternoon of Thursday, the 14th. This information is derived from Wardour's own statement.

"A number of people know of the existence of the pistol, and where it was kept. Among them was Dredger. It would have been a simple matter for any one to have entered Wardour's house during his absence and abstract the pistol.

"On the other hand, there is no evidence that it was stolen. Wardour himself may have taken it and given it to some other person."

Arnold considered these points for a few moments, then glanced at the clock. It was still early in the afternoon. He picked up a directory, and looked up the Yates' telephone number. On putting a call through, and giving his name, he was informed that Mr. Yates would see him.

Half an hour later he was seated in the lawyer's office in Coleman Street. "I am investigating the death of your client, Sir Wilfred Saxonby," he said, when he had introduced himself. "As you are aware, it appears on the surface to be a case of suicide. But certain facts have come to the knowledge of the police, making it possible that this assumption is incorrect."

The lawyer looked at him keenly. "So I guessed, when I learnt that the inquest had been adjourned," he replied. "I will not embarrass you by asking for an account of those facts. But I should like to say this. I have an intimate knowledge of my late client's private affairs, and I know of no circumstance which might have induced him to take his own life. Of the conduct of his business I know very little. But if he had any worries from that direction I have failed to find any indication of them."

"Thank you, Mr. Yates. The alternative to suicide can only be murder. I should naturally like to know who may be said to benefit by Sir Wilfred's death?"

"His will is a very simple document. There are legacies to the staff of Wigland and Bunthorne, and to the domestic staff at Mavis Court, on a sliding scale, according to length of service. This scale is, in my opinion, exceedingly generous. There are a few bequests to charities in which my client was interested. Miss Olivia Saxonby receives the sum of twenty-five thousand pounds, free of duty, as a reward for her companionship. Mavis Court and its contents fall to Richard, the son of the testator. The remainder of the estate, which, I anticipate, will be proved at nearly half a million, is divided between the said Richard and his sister, Mrs. Wardour, in equal shares."

"Would retired members of the staff share in the legacies equally with those still serving?" Arnold asked.

"Certainly. An employee of the firm who had retired after forty years' service would benefit to the extent of five hundred pounds. Mrs. Wardour informs me that this is the case of the late manager of the Manchester office, whose name for the moment escapes me."

It had not escaped Arnold, who refrained, however, from supplying the deficiency of Mr. Yates' memory. It was remarkable how Mr. Dredger kept coming up! But there was another point upon which the inspector felt a certain curiosity. "Mrs. Wardour, I am informed, is not on terms of complete harmony with her husband," he said. "This was a source of some disappointment to Sir Wilfred, was it not?"

"To some extent, yes," the lawyer replied. "He did his best to reconcile them, but without effect. He was fond of his daughter, and he had a genuine regard for Major Wardour. He could never understand why they didn't get on better together. I could have told him. They are both too masterful. Mrs. Wardour takes after her father in that respect."

Arnold smiled. "Just one thing more, Mr. Yates," he said. "During the afternoon of Thursday, Sir Wilfred received a visitor at his office, who gave the name of Yates. Did you or your son communicate with him that day?"

"No, we did not. My son and I were engaged together upon a very important matter that afternoon, and neither of us left this office until after six. Nor did we have any occasion to communicate with Saxonby for at least a week before his death."

"It has been suggested that Sir Wilfred, at the time of his death, may have had some object of value in his possession. Have you any reason to believe that this might have been the case?"

The lawyer shook his head. "None whatever," he replied. "I know of no such object, nor, up to the present, have I come across any reference to it in his private papers. That suggestion, I take it, has been put forward as an explanation of the possibility of murder?"

"Yes. If Sir Wilfred was murdered, the action was deliberate, and there must have been some motive behind it. Can you offer any suggestion, Mr. Yates?"

"Of why anybody should have wanted to murder Saxonby? That opens a very large question, Inspector. The provocation to murder varies in degree with different persons. Although Saxonby was not generally popular, owing to his rather overbearing manner, I cannot imagine any of his friends or acquaintances receiving such provocation that the only course open to them was murder. On the other hand, members of a certain class of society might consider that they had sufficient grievance to justify such an act."

"I am afraid that I do not quite follow you, Mr. Yates. To what class do you refer?"

"The class which appears in the police courts. Saxonby, as you are no doubt aware, was the chairman of the local bench. It is not for me to criticise him in that capacity beyond remarking that on occasions he appeared reluctant to temper justice with mercy."

This aspect of the matter had not occurred to Arnold. He made a mental note to discuss it with Marden, next time they met. Then, after thanking the lawyer for his information, he took his departure.

XIII

BEFORE ATTEMPTING TO ARRANGE THESE FURTHER FACTS IN their proper places, Arnold decided to pay one more call. He took the tube to Hampstead and went to Mrs. Wardour's house. On presenting his card, he was informed that Mrs. Wardour was at home and would see him.

He would have had no difficulty in recognising her as Sir Wilfred's daughter. Her features resembled his, and she had that typical hardness of expression which seemed to be a characteristic of the Saxonby family. She received Arnold without any surprise.

"I have heard of you before, Inspector," she said. "You have been down to Mavis Court, inquiring about my father's death, I believe?"

"That is correct, Mrs. Wardour," Arnold replied. "Now I am going to invoke your help in my investigation."

"You are welcome to what help I can give you, but I know very little about the matter, since I was abroad at the time. But of one thing I'm perfectly certain. My father never shot himself, whatever people may say."

"Would you mind telling me what makes you so certain?"

"My knowledge of my father's character, and of his views upon suicide. It was a subject upon which he felt very strongly. He held that suicide, under any circumstances whatever, was a crime unpardonable both in this world and the next. Besides, even if he had acted against his principles, a thing which I have never known him do, there was absolutely nothing to make him wish to end his life."

"He had no worries with regard to business, Mrs. Wardour?"

"The business has never been so flourishing as it is now, and everything is running perfectly smoothly. I can assure you that he can have had no worries, whether about business or anything else."

There was a short pause before Arnold spoke again. "You realise that the alternative to suicide is a very grave one, Mrs. Wardour?"

"Of course I do. My father was murdered. I realised that as soon as I heard what had happened. And I expect the police to bring his murderer to justice."

"They will do their best, you may rest assured of that. But can you give me any reason why any one should have murdered Sir Wilfred?"

"I would not have believed that anybody would have done such a thing. No doubt you are aware that several people will benefit by my father's will?"

"You refer, no doubt, to his employees?"

Mrs. Wardour shrugged her shoulders impatiently. "Oh, yes, they get a few small sums, of course. But there is one person who gets a legacy out of all proportion. How my father was persuaded into such a thing, I can't imagine."

"Who is that person, Mrs. Wardour?" Arnold asked innocently.

"My cousin Olivia. Twenty-five thousand pounds! Why, it's monstrous! My father burdens himself with a girl who is practically a pauper, gives her a home and keeps her in every luxury, and then, when he dies, leaves her all that money. What Richard will say when he hears of it, I don't know."

"Surely you are not suggesting that Miss Olivia had anything to do with your father's death?"

"I don't suppose that she shot him herself, if that's what you mean. But Olivia is deeper than you'd think. Of course, she wheedled my father into putting that clause in his will. And she's quite capable of having got round somebody else to shoot him. You don't know her as well as I do, Inspector."

"Not yet, Mrs. Wardour. Now, what can you tell me about Mr. Dredger, the late manager of the Manchester office of your firm?"

It appeared that Mrs. Wardour knew all about Mr. Dredger. But she could tell Arnold nothing that he had not already learnt from other sources. But her suspicions were evidently aroused. "What made you ask me about Mr. Dredger?" she asked.

"Oh, I happened to hear his name mentioned as having received a substantial legacy. He paid a visit to Major Wardour not long ago, did he not?"

"Yes, he did. But what on earth has that got to do with it?"

"Probably nothing. But Major Wardour showed him a pistol on that occasion. You have seen the weapon yourself, I have no doubt, Mrs. Wardour?"

"Oh, yes. I've seen it. He keeps it in a drawer of his desk. I've often asked him to get rid of it, but he never would. My husband is not the sort of man to be trusted with a pistol. He's got the most abominable temper, and I'm always afraid that he'll threaten somebody with it, or even shoot them. I spoke to my father about it once, and he promised to do what he could. Whether he spoke to Stephen or not, I don't know, but if he did, nothing came of it."

Arnold had no more questions to put to Mrs. Wardour. He returned to Scotland Yard, made a few additional notes, and then went home.

On reaching his office in the morning he found a letter awaiting him from the police at Blackdown. Inquiries had been made locally and a witness had been found who remembered seeing Mr. Dredger on the previous Thursday. This was a bus conductor, working on the route between Blackdown and Medbridge. He knew both Mr. Dredger and his daughter-in-law. On Thursday, just before half-past twelve, his bus had reached the turning leading to Little Hazelbury, on its journey from Medbridge to Blackdown. Mr. Dredger was standing at the corner. He stopped the bus and got in, and travelled as far as Blackdown railway station.

Acting upon this information, the police had interviewed the Dredgers' maid. Her statement was to the effect that Mrs. Dredger had gone away hastily on Thursday morning, she believed as a result of a telegram she had received. She had not returned until the following evening. Not long after her departure Mr. Dredger had gone out, she supposed in his car. He had returned just after one o'clock, but she could not say whether he had brought back the car or not. The garage could not be seen from the house. The maid had gone out about two o'clock. Mr. Dredger was then at home. She saw him again when she returned about ten.

This seemed to put Mr. Dredger's complicity in the affair beyond question. Clearly he had left his car at the ventilating shaft, walked back to the main road, taken a bus, and driven to the station. The times fitted in perfectly. Why had he gone to the station? Because it was a convenient place for an appointment with one of his accomplices, to whom, no doubt, he reported that the car was in position. This done, he returned home at his usual hour for lunch.

A second message awaited Arnold's attention, this time from the police at Plymouth. A telegram addressed to Mrs. Dredger had been traced. It had been handed in at the General Post Office at Plymouth at 8.10 a.m. on the previous Thursday. The wording of the telegram was as follows: "Harold had serious accident come at once Fred." On the back of the telegram, in the space reserved for that purpose, was the name and address of the sender. "Figgis, Grand Hotel, Plymouth." The wording of the telegram was in block letters throughout.

Inquiries at the Grand Hotel had revealed that no person of the name of Figgis had been staying there at the time. The clerks at the post office had been questioned, but none of them could give any information as to the person who had handed in the telegram. Both Mrs. Dredger's nephew and his friend had been interviewed. They confirmed Mrs. Dredger's visit to Plymouth, but denied all knowledge of the telegram. There had been no accident.

This was confirmation of Mr. Dredger's statement, up to a point. A hoax had been perpetrated, but by whom? The telegram had obviously been sent to ensure Mrs. Dredger's absence from Blackdown on the previous Thursday. Her absence had been necessary to the scheme, since it was essential that Mr. Dredger's movements should not be observed by inquisitive eyes. To Arnold this was fresh evidence that every detail had been most carefully thought out beforehand. And there was no doubt that several people had been implicated. Was Dredger the mainspring of the conspiracy?

Before the inspector had answered this question to his own satisfaction, Merrion was announced. "Well, I got your message," he said. "Having nothing better to do, I came up at once. I gather that you've got some fresh light on this Saxonby case?"

"I've found the man who left the car at the ventilating shaft," Arnold replied. "But it's rather a long story. What if we go out and get some lunch, and I'll tell you what I've been doing since I saw you last."

During the meal, Arnold recounted his adventures, beginning with his second visit to the offices of Wigland and Bunthorne, and ending with the two messages which he had received that morning. "Well," he concluded, "and now let's have your comments. You'll observe, by the way, that your theory of the substitution of the wallets falls to the ground. The notes found on Sir Wilfred had been issued to him a few hours before by his own cashier."

Merrion laughed. "What I like about this case is the delicate balance of evidence," he replied. "To begin with, there is at least as much evidence in support of the theory of suicide as there is against it. You say that the fact that the pistol did not belong to Saxonby, but to his son-in-law, is conclusive proof that he was murdered. But it isn't. By your own showing, that pistol may have fallen into anybody's hands. Why not those of Saxonby, who was one of the people who had seen the pistol, and knew where it was kept?

"But I won't labour that point. Let's concentrate upon the wallet. This is the evidence in favour of my theory of substitution. First, Miss Olivia Saxonby swears that the wallet found in her uncle's pocket is not the one with which he left home. That, to my mind, is pretty convincing. Then comes the fact that it contained neither the railway ticket nor the letter from Mrs. Wardour. You didn't ask her about that letter, I gather?"

"No. I didn't want to say too much to her, since it seems to me more than likely that her husband is implicated."

"I see. Now for the evidence against the substitution. Torrance is pretty certain that the wallet found in Saxonby's pocket is the one he habitually used. But then he knew nothing of the stitches which had been put in the lining. We only have Miss Saxonby's unsupported statement for those stitches, by the way. Again, you make that point about the five-pound notes. Why change the wallets, if their contents or some of them had to be changed? And, if they were changed, somebody must have gone to some considerable trouble to secure a second wallet, exactly like the first. Summed up in that way, I think you'll agree that the evidence is pretty evenly balanced. Now, was there an interchange of wallets, or was there not?"

"I'm inclined to think that there wasn't," Arnold replied.

"And I think there was. I've stated the evidence on both sides, impartially, as you must admit. Now let's examine it. Miss Olivia Saxonby's statement to begin with. She, apparently very much to Mrs. Wardour's annoyance, comes in for twenty-five thousand under her uncle's will. In considering what reliance can be placed upon her statements, that fact must not be lost sight of. But why on earth should she have fabricated that story of the stitches, if it wasn't true? If she knows anything about the affair, it is the very last thing which she would have done. It would be in her interest to prove that no exchange of wallets had taken place, thus supporting the suicide theory. Instead of which she deliberately, and of her own accord, declares that an exchange had been made. This being so, I prefer her evidence to Torrance's.

"Not that I mean to cast any slur upon Torrance's veracity. Wallet number two is exactly similar in external appearance to number one. We have Miss Saxonby's word for that. It is only that he has never handled number one, and therefore he has probably never seen the lining. He judges by outward appearance only, a tendency to which all of us are liable. The five-pound notes suggest an even more delicate point. You consider them to be conclusive evidence against an exchange of wallets. With all deference, I take an entirely opposite view. I believe that they form conclusive evidence that the wallets were changed."

"Why, how on earth do you make that out?" Arnold exclaimed.

"It's that vivid imagination of mine again. Let me run over the sequence of events. According to the cashier it was on Thursday *morning* that Saxonby cashed his cheque and received the notes. In the afternoon he received this mysterious visitor, whom nobody seems able to identify. Now suppose that for some reason, which we can't yet attempt to fathom, Saxonby gave his visitor those notes. The visitor puts them in wallet number two, knowing that it will be possible to trace them to Saxonby, and thus fabricating what you consider a valuable piece of evidence."

"Ingenious, but without any shadow of proof," Arnold remarked. "But, after all, the question of the wallets is a minor one..."

"Don't you believe it," Merrion interrupted. "However, carry on."

"The main question is, who killed Sir Wilfred? The man we call A, who travelled from Cannon Street by the five o'clock train, and, we suppose, left it in Blackdown Tunnel. But who is A? He answers to the description of Dredger, who undoubtedly played some part in the business. But I've seen Dredger, who is anything but an active man. And I don't believe that he is capable of the necessary gymnastic feats.

"Was A Major Wardour? There's no doubt that the pistol is his. He reached London at half-past three on Thursday afternoon, and made no statement which could be checked of his movements subsequently. If A was not Dredger, he was made up to look like him. Wardour admits having met Dredger once, and may very likely have met him secretly several times. If so, he knew what he looked like, and would be able to assume the appropriate disguise."

"Hold on a minute," said Merrion. "I'd like to make a few observations before you go any further. I agree with you that it is extremely improbable that A was Dredger, for the reason you state. And yet you say that Dredger played some part in the business, that in other words he was an accomplice. Wouldn't it have been rather a dirty trick on A's part to disguise himself as one of his own accomplices?"

"Not if the accomplice was in a position to prove that he didn't commit the murder. In that case it would be rather a neat dodge."

"But Dredger can't prove that he didn't commit the murder, that's just the point. Owing to an extraordinary combination of circumstances, his movements were unobserved during the whole of that afternoon and evening. My next point is this. You think that Wardour may have been A. It certainly seems possible. But the really careful murderer doesn't leave lying about a pistol which can be traced back to him."

"He thought that it would be assumed to be Sir Wilfred's," Arnold replied. "However, that doesn't exhaust the possibilities. A may have been any other person, the man who gave his name as Yates, for instance. But, whoever it was, he must have known Dredger very well, since he got himself up to look like him. It all comes back to Dredger, whichever way you look at it."

"Yes, poor old Dredger seems to be the centre of attraction. This case of yours seems to get more and more involved, the further you go. Have you formed any theory, to use as a working basis, so to speak?"

"I've accepted your theory as to what happened in the tunnel and above it. Sir Wilfred was murdered by A, who was subsequently hauled up the shaft by B. I'm not clear about the motive for the murder, but there seems to have been a conspiracy against Sir Wilfred, in which Dredger, Wardour, the man known as Yates, and almost certainly others were involved. We know the part played by Dredger..."

"We don't, you know," Merrion interrupted. "You're putting too much faith in the farmer and the bus conductor. Apparently you are prepared to admit that A purposely disguised himself as Dredger in the afternoon. Why shouldn't he have done so in the morning?"

"But, dash it all, there's that telegram from Plymouth! You're not going to suggest that the hoax played upon Mrs. Dredger had nothing to do with the affair? That its occurrence on the day of Sir Wilfred's death was a sheer coincidence?"

"Of course I'm not. But let me propound a theory of my own. What do we know of the murderer? Quite a lot. We have already agreed that he was intimately acquainted with Saxonby. His ability to produce an almost exact replica of the wallet proves that, apart from anything else. I'm still convinced, you see, that the wallet is the crux of the affair. Why should not his intimacy extend to Saxonby's family and his business associates?

"Admitting that this is likely, and, in fact, probable, it follows that the murderer may well have known both Major Wardour and Mr. Dredger. It was common knowledge that the former had a pistol, upon which was engraved a monogram S.W., which could as easily be read W.S. It was also common knowledge that Dredger lived at Blackdown, conveniently near the tunnel. The murderer was already familiar with his appearance, and knew how to get himself up to resemble him sufficiently to pass muster with strangers. The test of resemblance was only submitted to strangers, or comparative strangers. Mrs. Wardour, for instance, would probably not have been deceived for a moment.

"Now our murderer is determined to take no risks of discovery. He stages his crime so that it shall appear to be a case of suicide. And very ably he does so. Had it not been for Inspector Arnold of the Yard, a verdict of suicide would have been returned, and the matter would have blown over. But, not content with that, he establishes a second line of defence. He impersonates a wholly innocent person, whose habits and residence near the scene of the crime was suitable to his purpose. And he contrives that that person shall not be in a position to prove his innocence."

"According to you, then, Dredger was born under an unlucky star," Arnold remarked sceptically.

"He was. Now, let's see if we can't follow the murderer's movements. I'm going to call him A once more, for convenience. He has, no doubt, studied Dredger and his habits. He is familiar with the make and appearance of his car, and knows that it is fitted with a set of fairly new Dunlop tyres. He provides himself with an exactly similar car, not a very difficult matter. He knows that Dredger is in the habit of pottering round in his car in the mornings. So he carries out his preliminaries, involving the apparent breakdown of the car at the shaft, and then takes a bus to Blackdown station, secure in the knowledge that if anybody notices him they will take him for Dredger. He has arranged for Mrs. Dredger to be out of the way. I suspect B's hand in that telegram.

"Before we make any further conjecture as to A's identity, let me point out something that strikes me as rather curious. We have mentioned it before, but not in the light of what we know now. A was intimately acquainted, not only with Saxonby, but with Dredger also. In addition, he knew about Wardour's pistol. Who do you suppose fulfils these conditions?"

"Sir Wilfred's son and daughter, who were directors of the firm. And possibly the more confidential members of the staff."

"Exactly. And of these, at the time of the crime, the son was in America, the daughter in the south of France, and Torrance, as secretary of the firm and the most confidential of the lot, one would suppose, either in Manchester or on his way back from there. And their absences were all due to Saxonby's own suggestion. That's what I can't get over.

"But, in the absence of these people, there is one individual who seems to have been at least on fairly intimate terms with Saxonby. He calls at his office, where he is unknown to the staff. He gives the name of the solicitor who looks after Saxonby's private affairs. He has an appointment, and is immediately admitted to Saxonby's presence. Who was this man, and what was his business?

"It was after his visit that Saxonby took the unusual precautions of a taxi to Cannon Street and a carriage to himself in the train. What can have passed between them? I still adhere to my theory that Yates, as we must call him, brought Saxonby some article of value, and received those three five-pound notes in exchange. And I will go still further, I will suggest that Saxonby knew well in advance that Yates would come and see him last Thursday. Did he send away his son, his daughter and his secretary so that his visitor should not be seen by prying eyes?"

Arnold laughed. "I've never known you at a loss for a theory," he replied. "But if Sir Wilfred didn't want Yates to be seen, wouldn't it have been simpler to have fixed the appointment at Mavis Court?"

"Under the watchful eyes of Miss Olivia Saxonby and the servants? No, I think not. However that may be, let us see if A and Yates can be made to fit together. Yates, as Dredger, plays his part at Blackdown in the morning. He then goes to the station and takes a train to London, removing the Dredger disguise en route, perhaps. He appears at the office in his own semblance. He reassumes his disguise and takes his seat in the five o'clock train. It fits in all right, you see."

"Yes, it fits in all right," Arnold replied reluctantly. "But..."

"Oh, yes, I know. We're a long way yet from proving a case against Yates. But I feel pretty certain of one thing. Find out what his business was with Saxonby and you've gone a long way towards solving the problem."

XIV

THAT EVENING, WHEN MERRION WAS ALONE IN HIS ROOMS, HE set his mind to work systematically upon the problem of Sir Wilfred Saxonby's death. He felt it quite safe to assume that he had been murdered. But by whom, and for what reason?

To take the first part of the question. Saxonby had been shot by the man known as A, who had travelled in the five o'clock train in the guise of Mr. Dredger. This man had an accomplice, B, who had carried out the necessary operations at the top of the ventilating shaft. One or other of these men, or possibly both, had an intimate knowledge of Saxonby's affairs, of his family and business.

As to the motive, Merrion still adhered to his theory of a valuable object. It need not necessarily have been of intrinsic value, it might merely have had a special value in the eyes of the murderer. It had probably been handed over to Saxonby by the man calling himself Yates. Considerable secrecy had attached to the transaction, since Yates' visit had taken place when Saxonby had deliberately sent his son, his daughter, and his secretary out of the way. Probably nobody had known of the purport of the visit but Yates and Saxonby. Yates, having handed over the object, had determined to get it back again, and had made his plans for doing so in advance. And, since Saxonby would not willingly relinquish it, the only course open to Yates was to murder him.

This seemed to Merrion a plausible theory, if not correct in detail, at least good enough to work upon. What suggestions did it afford of clues which might be followed up?

First of all, the breakdown lorry. It was a type of vehicle which, though common, was limited in numbers. Only garages, and fairly big garages at that, possessed such lorries. It might be possible to take a census of them and to find out how each was employed on the previous Thursday. Scotland Yard might invite the police throughout the country to make the necessary inquiries.

Next, the visit of Yates to the offices of Wigland and Bunthorne. On the surface this had appeared simple enough. An acquaintance of Saxonby's had made an appointment to see him, ostensibly upon some private matter. He had come, stayed a few minutes, and left again. There was nothing at all out of the way in that. But why the secrecy with which the visit had been surrounded? The only possible answer seemed to be that Saxonby's son or daughter, or Torrance, would have recognised Yates. And Saxonby had his own reasons for concealing the visit from them.

Merrion had not forgotten that ammunition which fitted the pistol had been found in Saxonby's filing cabinet. This fact had strengthened the suggestion of suicide. It seemed to show that Saxonby had kept the pistol and ammunition in the cabinet, and had loaded the pistol and taken it with him on his departure from the office. On the other hand, if Saxonby had been murdered, and the ammunition was part of that taken from Wardour's store, how had it found its way into the cabinet?

The evidence regarding the cabinet was by no means conclusive. According to Torrance it was always kept locked, only Saxonby had access to it, and he alone possessed a key to fit it. But Merrion was sufficiently experienced to be sceptical in such matters. Torrance's statement had been made in perfectly good faith, no doubt. But duplicate keys could be made. Besides, the cabinet wasn't always kept locked. It had been found unlocked on the morning after Saxonby's death. Absent-mindedness on his part, no doubt. But what evidence was there that this was the first time that such a thing had happened? It might have been left unlocked on some former occasion, and advantage taken of this to slip the cartridges into it.

All this was possible. But Merrion's imagination evolved an alternative theory. Yates, if he were the murderer, must have obtained possession of the pistol before his visit to Saxonby. With the pistol he had taken a supply of cartridges. During the interview Saxonby had perhaps opened the cabinet, in order to refer to some document among its contents. It would not have been difficult for Yates to have slipped in the cartridges then.

Next, as to his acquisition of the pistol and cartridges. He must have known that Wardour possessed such a weapon, and where he kept it. He must have been familiar with Wardour's house, and known of his absence abroad. In fact, everything pointed to his being a friend of Wardour's. And it was certain that he was intimately acquainted with Saxonby. How did it happen, then, that he was a complete stranger to the staff in Saxonby's office?

And then Merrion had an inspiration. Hitherto he had concentrated his attention upon Yates, to the neglect of his accomplice. But what if the accomplice had been the originator of the plot? What if he had made all the arrangements, and supplied Yates with the pistol?

What was known of this accomplice, B? Next to nothing. Nobody had so much as seen him. But he must have existed, as the arrival at the shaft of the breakdown lorry proved. Could he have been Wardour himself?

There seemed no practical reason why he should not have been. Yates' secret, whatever it was, might have been known to him. The two might have agreed to murder Saxonby for the sake of the mysterious object. On the whole, Wardour seemed to fit the bill quite comfortably. He would, obviously, be familiar with his father-in-law's habits. He would know by which train he almost invariably travelled. He would be sufficiently acquainted with his wallet to provide one exactly similar. But once more the question arose. Would he have provided his colleague with his own pistol?

The complexities of the problem were maddening. The impersonation of Dredger, for example. That was highly ingenious, but it had been carried too far. Merrion would have been prepared to believe that Dredger had driven his car to the shaft and left it there. That was within the power of a man of his age and infirmity. But to suppose that he had been the passenger in the five o'clock train was ridiculous. He could not have carried out that surprising feat in the tunnel. And since, therefore, he had been impersonated then, he could just as easily have been impersonated in the morning.

But the impersonation was in itself a clue. For one of the conspirators, A or B, must have been familiar with his habits. Not only that, but he must have known of the existence of those bright lads Harold and Fred, and of Mrs. Dredger's affection for the former. Who could be imagined to possess this knowledge, in addition to that already stipulated? Only somebody connected with the firm of Wigland and Bunthorne, surely. Mrs. Wardour, for instance, who seemed to take a particular interest in Dredger. Had she not suggested his visit to her husband's poultry farm?

Could Mrs. Wardour have organised the affair, and then retired gracefully to the South of France while it was being carried out? It seemed an altogether fantastic idea, though not entirely outside the bounds of possibility. She had known all about the pistol, admitted having spoken of it to her father. She had told Arnold that her husband was not the sort of man to be trusted with a pistol. Was she trying to throw suspicion upon him? They appeared, from all accounts, to be at loggerheads. But, Merrion repeated, she must be the very devil of a woman if she engineered the murder of her father and then did her best to get her husband hanged for the crime.

Next morning, Merrion called at Scotland Yard, prepared to share his ideas with Arnold. But as soon as he mentioned the breakdown lorry, he found that the inspector had forestalled him. "Oh, that's a matter of almost automatic routine!" said Arnold. "We sent out a request for information from all the local police forces, days ago, and reports are beginning to come in. Here's a pile of them which came in this morning. I was just going to run through them. You can lend a hand, if you like."

They proceeded to examine the reports, which were disappointingly negative, until they came to one originating from Plymouth. A second-hand breakdown lorry had been purchased at an auction in the town during the month of October. It had been driven away by its new owner on the evening of November 13th, and had not since been heard of. Further inquiries would be made if desired.

"We've heard of Plymouth before," said Arnold thoughtfully. "It's where Dredger's daughter-in-law's nephew lives. Wonderful how Dredger's name crops up, whichever way we turn. I've half a mind to run down to Plymouth myself and have a look round."

"I don't mind coming with you," Merrion replied. "If we look sharp we can just catch the 10.30 from Paddington. What about it?"

Arnold agreed. They took a taxi, and were just in time to catch the train. During the journey Merrion mentioned the other points which had occurred to him, without producing any very great impression upon Arnold, who seemed to have Dredger on the brain. "He holds the key to the whole affair," he said. "It's all very fine to say that somebody else impersonated him, but you've got to find that person. I've half a mind to arrest the chap on suspicion, and see if a taste of the cells won't make him speak."

"You must please yourself," Merrion replied. "It doesn't strike me as very good policy, though. Have him watched, by all means. But, if it turns out that he really was in the plot, his arrest will be the sequel for everybody else concerned to make themselves scarce. Better see where this clue of the lorry leads to before you decide."

On arriving at Plymouth they called upon the local constabulary, where they were informed that the information forwarded had been obtained from the manager of the Celtic Garage. They found this to be a large establishment on the outskirts of the town, which seemed to be doing a prosperous trade. The manager, to whom they introduced themselves, offered them every assistance. "I'm anxious to find the fellow who drove that lorry away, for my own reasons," he said. "He's got a set of my trade number plates, and he's never returned them. But I'd better tell you the whole story.

"For some years now we have held a quarterly sale by auction of used cars on our premises. As I dare say you know, when we sell a new car we nearly always have to take an old one in part exchange, and the problem of getting rid of these is enough to drive one to drink. The best of them we manage, sooner or later, to sell privately, but there's always a lot of junk left over. And these we sell by auction without reserve, simply for the sake of getting them out of the way.

"Now, as it happened, last October we had a breakdown lorry to dispose of. It was our own and had been in use for a couple of years, but we found it hardly powerful enough for our purpose. In a hilly country like this we wanted something with more guts in it. So we bought another and advertised the old one for sale. But nobody seemed to want it, and I decided to put it into the auction with the rest.

"It fetched quite a good price, rather more than I expected. And when the sale was over, the young fellow who had bought it came to see me. He told me that he owned a garage in a small way near London, and had found it time to get a breakdown lorry. But he had nowhere to put it until an extension which he was having built was finished. Would I mind storing the lorry for a week or two? He would be quite ready to pay any reasonable sum for the privilege. He seemed quite a decent young fellow, and I told him the lorry could stay where it was until he was ready. And, if he had no objection to our using it in case of emergency, if we got an urgent call when the new lorry was out, for example, we wouldn't charge him anything. He was perfectly satisfied with this arrangement, and he gave me his card. I've got it in my pocket now."

The manager produced the card and gave it to Arnold. Upon it was printed:

THE BLACKDOWN GARAGE,
LONDON ROAD,
BLACKDOWN.

MR. WILLIAM FIGGIS.

Arnold made no comment, but passed the card to Merrion, with a triumphant glance. Then he turned to the manager. "Mr. Figgis collected the lorry later, I understand?"

"He came here on the evening of Wednesday, November 13th, and told me he had come to take his lorry away. And then a difficulty cropped up. The lorry wasn't registered. We had never registered it, for whenever it went out it did so with our trade number plates. Figgis ought to have realised this when he bought it, but apparently he hadn't. So there we were. The lorry couldn't go out unregistered, and it was too late then to take out a registration. Figgis was terribly upset. He said it was absolutely necessary that he should be in Blackdown by the following morning. At last, since he was in the trade, and we all try to help one another as much as we can, I took pity on him. I said that he could drive the lorry home under a set of our trade number plates, on the strict understanding that he sent back the plates by passenger train the first thing next morning. This he promised to do. But the plates have never turned up, and from that day to this I've heard nothing of Mr. Figgis."

"You must have communicated with him, surely?" Arnold asked.

"I've tried to. I wrote to him on Thursday morning, telling him that the plates had not been received, and asking him to send them back without delay. I sent the letter to the address on his card, and it came back 'Not known.' Apart from my being short of a pair of number plates, it strikes me that there is something pretty queer about all this."

"I'm inclined to agree with you," said Arnold. "Are you quite sure that Figgis left Plymouth with the lorry that evening?"

"He started, anyhow, for I sent one of my chaps with him to show him the best way out of the town. And also, for that matter, in case one of the local police should see a stranger driving under our number plates."

Merrion had an idea. "Is that chap of yours about?" he asked.

"Yes, I'll send for him," the manager replied. In due course the chap appeared, round-faced, and betraying no marked symptoms of intelligence.

"Do you remember going out with the gentleman who took away the old breakdown lorry, Tom?" the manager asked. "Wednesday evening last week, you know."

"Aye, I mind it well enough," Tom replied. "I went with him out to the Plough, on the Exeter road. And then he said he could find his way all right, and I came back by bus."

"Always a good plan to stop at a pub," Merrion remarked brightly. "He stood you a drink for your trouble, I hope?"

Tom gazed at him sulkily. "I won't deny we had a drop of cider," he replied.

"Of course, perfectly natural," said Merrion softly. "And what else did he give you, Tom?"

The other seemed to resent this question. "I don't know what business that might be of yours," he replied.

It was clearly time for Arnold to take a hand. "Then I'll tell you," he replied sternly. "I am an inspector from Scotland Yard, and I'll trouble you to answer the questions put to you, without any nonsense."

At the very mention of Scotland Yard, Tom's face went pale. He seemed to imagine that he was liable to be clapped in gaol for the rest of his life, without chance of appeal. "I'm sure I beg pardon, sir," he stammered. "I wouldn't think for a moment of hiding anything from you. It's quite true that the gentleman did give me something else. It was in the Plough, while we were having our cider. He said that he had just remembered that he had a telegram which he meant to send before he left the town. And he asked me if I would send it for him first thing next morning on my way to work. I said I would, and he gave me the telegram and the money for it, and half a quid."

"Did you read the telegram?" Arnold asked.

"No, sir. I shouldn't have thought of doing that. Besides, the gentleman said it was private, and asked me not to say anything to anybody else."

"Oh, he did, did he? And what did you do with the telegram?"

"I told the gentleman that there would be plenty of time to hand it in that evening, when I got back to the town. But he said no, he didn't want that. So I handed it at the General Post Office next morning on my way to work."

Arnold turned to the manager. "Can you describe this man Figgis?" he asked.

"Fairly tall and rather slightly built. Fair, clean-shaven, with rather a pleasant face which might be called good-looking. Quite young, not more than thirty at the most. And very well dressed. In fact, that was the first thing I noticed about him. In the course of conversation he told me that he had been an actor, but that there was no money in it. So, having come into a little capital a couple of years ago, he had opened a garage and was doing very well."

Tom corroborated the manager's description, adding the further particular that Figgis "spoke like a real gentleman." Arnold and Merrion, having secured minute particulars of the lorry, left the garage and went back to the police station. It had occurred to both of them that Figgis might turn out to be Dredger's relative Harold, or perhaps his comrade-in-arms, Fred. With the help of the local police they ran these two young gentlemen to earth. But they had no difficulty in proving, beyond possibility of doubt, that neither of them could be the wanted man.

On their way back to London in the night train Arnold and Merrion discussed the lorry and the identity of the elusive Figgis. "It's no use trying to pretend now that Dredger isn't in some way mixed up in this," Arnold maintained doggedly. "Look at this chap Figgis, who gives the address of a garage which doesn't exist. What address does he give? London Road, Blackdown! Dredger lives in London Road, Blackdown? Do you mean to tell me that's sheer coincidence? Nonsense!"

"I didn't tell you anything of the kind," replied Merrion mildly.

"No, but you thought it. Besides, how did Figgis know about Harold and Fred, if Dredger didn't tell him, eh?"

"Never mind about Dredger for the moment. He won't run away. Let's see if we can make anything of this lorry business. To begin with, we have evidence that the crime was planned some time ago. Figgis bought the lorry as early as last month. That may turn out to be a useful piece of information. Next, Figgis did not collect it until the day before it was wanted. Clearly, I think, because he did not want to be seen in possession of such an unusual vehicle as a breakdown lorry. Whatever he may be by profession, I don't suppose he's a garage proprietor. And for anybody else to own such a thing might excite remark.

"Then that dodge of borrowing a set of trade number plates from the Celtic Garage. That was a pretty cute move. It saved him the necessity of registering the lorry, also from providing a clue by which he might have been traced. And I haven't a doubt that he was still using those number plates on Thursday evening. If any one had seen him, and made a note of the number, this would have been traced to the Celtic Garage, and we should be no further than we are now."

"And that's not very far," Arnold grumbled. "We know where the lorry came from, and quite a lot about its past history. All very interesting, no doubt, but it doesn't help us to lay hands on the man who murdered Sir Wilfred. Where is the lorry now? That's what we want to know."

"Not very far from Blackdown, I expect," replied Merrion thoughtfully.

"And Dredger knows where it could be found, I'll wager."

"Oh, darn Dredger! Can't you try to forget him for a minute or two? I've two reasons, entirely unconnected with him, for supposing that either A or B live near Blackdown. The first takes us back to that dodge of the lights in the tunnel. Before that could even have been thought of, the existence of the shaft must have been known. And that presupposes local knowledge, for it is not in any way conspicuous, and is most unlikely to be discovered by a stranger.

"And then, when it had been decided to make use of the shaft, a lot of research must have been necessary. Somebody must have made a lot of very careful observations. I need only mention a few. He would have to find out what time the five o'clock from Cannon Street ran through Blackdown station. Since it does not stop there, that is not mentioned in the ordinary time-table. He would also have to observe the time taken by the train to travel from the entrance of the tunnel to the shaft. He would have to make sure that no up train ran through the tunnel at the same time. These are only a few of the things he had to find out, and he could only do so by local observation."

"Dredger could have..." Arnold began, but Merrion stopped him peremptorily. "If you mention that man's name again, I shall do something rash. I don't say that there isn't the possibility that he had something to do with it. But can't you keep an open mind, without trying to twist everything to that conclusion?

"Now for my second reason. Plymouth, I suppose, is approximately two hundred and forty miles from Blackdown. Figgis, we are told, left Plymouth about half-past five on Wednesday evening. Naturally, he would not be anxious to parade the lorry before the eyes of the public during the hours of daylight. And that raises rather an interesting point. He would not want the lorry to be on the road between, roughly, the hours of sunrise and sunset on Thursday.

"We are told that he reached the shaft round about five o'clock on Thursday afternoon. Now, if he didn't want to drive in daylight, he can't have come very far. The sun set that day at 4.11 p.m. That gave him three-quarters of an hour, more or less, for his journey. Considerably less, I expect, for he would not want to start until it was really dusk. Therefore, there is reason to believe that, during the hours of daylight on Thursday, the lorry was hidden in some spot within ten miles of the shaft. That spot could have been reached during Wednesday night and the early hours of Thursday morning, even if the average speed during the journey from Plymouth was not more than twenty miles an hour."

"That sounds reasonable enough," Arnold remarked, rather grudgingly.

"It's perfectly reasonable. I won't make guesses about the situation of the spot, beyond suggesting that it would probably be waste of time to look for it in the centre of a town. The next point is this. Who is Figgis? You know as well as I do that a man who sets out to spin a tissue of lies very often shoves in a word of truth here and there, just to make his story more plausible. I wonder if Figgis was telling the truth when he told the manager of the Celtic Garage that he had been an actor?"

"Even if he was, it isn't much of a clue. You don't suppose that Figgis is his real name, do you?"

"Not for an instant. But doesn't an actor associate himself in your mind with the idea of disguise? The passenger seen by Mrs. and Miss Clutsam in the five o'clock train was certainly disguised. Even you can't really suppose that he was the individual whom we've agreed not to mention. Is it wildly improbable that this man, A, was really Figgis?"

"I thought you had already made up your mind he was Yates," Arnold replied sourly.

"And why shouldn't Yates and Figgis be one and the same?" Merrion retorted. "There is already a certain similarity between their descriptions. Yates, who visited the office of Wigland and Bunthorne on Thursday afternoon, and Figgis, who imposed upon the good nature of the garage manager on Wednesday evening, bear at least a family resemblance.

"Working on that theory, we learn a little more about the technique of the crime. A, or Figgis, buys the lorry. Still as Figgis, he goes down to Plymouth on Wednesday evening and drives it away. We know now that he took the opportunity of contriving the sending of the telegram which drew Mrs. Dredger from her accustomed haunts. During the early hours of Thursday morning he reaches a previously appointed rendezvous and leaves the lorry there.

"I suppose he then put in a few hours of well-earned sleep. His next appearance in the picture is about noon on Thursday, when, as Dredger—sorry, but the name slipped out unawares—he drives the small saloon car to the shaft and leaves it there. From the shaft he goes by bus to Blackdown station, and thence, we suppose, to London. He interviews Saxonby as Yates, a role needing no disguise. Finally, he travels in the five o'clock train in his disguise of the morning. All that is left for B is to collect the lorry from the rendezvous, drive it to the shaft, work the lights, and haul A out of the tunnel. His part is an easy one, compared with A's. Now, what does this curiously uneven distribution of parts suggest to you?"

"Why, that A was the principal and B merely an accomplice," replied Arnold. "That's obvious enough, surely?"

"A was certainly the actual murderer. But it doesn't follow that he was the organiser of the plot. I believe that he was allotted the greater part of the work for this reason. His movements were free from observation. B could not go about the country buying lorries, or leave cars by the wayside, without being asked awkward questions. And you'll notice this. B took on the delicate operations at the shaft. Doesn't that suggest that he was the person who had made the observations? If so, he lives near Blackdown. And again, if so, he probably provided the hiding-place for the lorry. And now, for heaven's sake, let's settle down and try to get a little sleep."

They relapsed into semi-slumber until their train drew into Paddington in the chill and unsympathetic dawn.

XV

Arnold was nothing if not methodical. His first action on reaching Scotland Yard was to make a summary of the description of the lorry, being careful to include the engine and chassis numbers, and all other relevant details. This he had manifolded and sent to all police stations within a wide radius of Blackdown, asking that a search should be made for a lorry answering to this description.

He was not very sanguine of obtaining any news. The lorry, having played its part, had probably been abandoned or destroyed. Or during Thursday night it might have been driven away many hundred miles from the scene of the crime. Still, once before, he had found the burnt-out remains of a lorry a very valuable clue, and there was just a chance that luck might be once more on his side. But he was more than surprised when, on the day after the issue of the description, he received a message that a lorry answering to it was in a wayside garage on the main London–Salisbury road, not far from Whitchurch in Hampshire.

He wasted no time in communicating with Merrion, but took the next train from Waterloo to Whitchurch. The garage, when he found it, turned out to be no more than a roadside filling-station, with a corrugated iron shed beside it. This modest establishment was owned by a middle-aged man of morose disposition, who appeared to augment his livelihood by keeping a number of bedraggled fowls. His name, it appeared, was Bleak.

In reply to Arnold's questions, he said that he had been in to Whitchurch that morning and had met the local policeman, who asked him if he had seen or heard anything of a stray breakdown lorry.

"Well, I said to him, that's a queer thing. I've one standing in my shed now. Not that you might call it a stray, for I'm expecting the chap as left it to come back and fetch it, any day."

"Who left it, and when?" Arnold asked.

"Nicely spoken chap, he was," Bleak replied. "Told me his name was Figgis and that he kept a garage at Blackdown. He'd been on the road for twenty-four hours and more and was fair fagged out. And so was the lorry, by all accounts. Anyway she wouldn't go any further, so he left her here. Said he was coming back in a day or two, but I haven't seen nothing of him since. Hasn't got that new carburettor from the makers yet, I reckon. Terrible time some of them keep you waiting for spare parts. Never seem to think that a man's got his living to earn."

All this was somewhat obscure to Arnold. "When did this man Figgis leave the lorry with you?" he asked.

"One evening last week, it was. Wednesday? No, it wasn't Wednesday, for that was the day my daughter was over to see me from Andover. Thursday, it must have been. Yes, Thursday it was, for it was the evening of the whist drive and dance at the Women's Institute. The missus had gone, but naturally I had to stop away. Somebody's got to be on hand to look after the petrol pumps."

"Yes, yes," said Arnold impatiently. "On Thursday evening, was it? What time?"

"Round about quarter to nine. I was sitting inside having a bite of supper when I heard a lorry pull up outside. The chap blew his horn, so I went out, thinking as how he'd be wanting a fill of petrol. And then I saw that it was one of them breakdown lorries. There was only one chap with it, and he got down from his seat and asked me where the nearest railway station was, and I told him Whitchurch, a couple of miles away. Then he asked what time the last train up to London was, and I told him nine forty-six. The chap looked at his watch and said that he reckoned he could do it comfortably.

"Then he told me who he was, and gave me his card. He said he had bought the lorry in Plymouth and had started to drive it back to his place on Wednesday evening. He hadn't got very far before his carburettor began to give trouble, and at last he had to stop for the night. In the morning he had taken it down and done the best he could with it, but he couldn't get it right, and he'd had trouble with it off and on all day. And now, he said, the blessed thing had packed up altogether, and he wouldn't trust it to go another dozen yards."

"Did he tell you where he had stopped the previous night?" Arnold asked.

"No, and I didn't ask him. It wasn't none of my business. He said that he had to be at his place first thing next morning, as he had a very important deal on hand. He'd have to leave the lorry and go on by train. He asked me if I had anywhere that he could put it, and I said there was room in my shed where I keeps the car that I use for hire-work. So he managed to get his lorry going again, and a terrible noise she made, spluttering and backfiring. But he managed to drive her into the shed, where she is now."

"Which direction had he come from?"

"Why, from Salisbury way, to be sure, seeing that he was coming from Plymouth. The other way runs through to Basingstoke and London. He had a pair of them red trade numbers on the car, and he took those off, saying that he'd want them. And then he said that the only thing to do was to send to the makers for a new carburettor and that as soon as he'd got it he'd come back and fix it and drive the lorry away. And then he went off carrying the number plates, to walk to Whitchurch and catch his train. And that's the last I've seen of him."

"What did he look like?"

"He seemed a decent young chap. Bit of a toff in his way, had a posh suit on, and that. Clean-shaven, he was, and nicely spoken, too. But you could tell that he'd a bit of trouble with the lorry for his face and hands was all black and dirty."

Arnold inspected the lorry and satisfied himself that it corresponded in every way with the description given to him in Plymouth. Then he investigated the interior of the body. He was rewarded by the discovery of a quantity of flexible cord, similar to the fragments which he and Merrion had found in Blackdown Tunnel. There was also a miscellaneous collection of electrical fittings, including a couple of switches.

Having warned Bleak that, if anybody came to fetch the lorry, he was not to let them have it but to communicate with the police at once, Arnold returned to Scotland Yard.

That evening he met Merrion and retailed to him his latest adventure. "And now that we've found the lorry, it doesn't lead us much farther," he concluded rather ruefully.

"Figgis didn't intend to leave any unnecessary clues," Merrion replied. "He's a pretty cunning devil, I'll say that for him. You notice how skilfully he blends the true and the false. He made no secret of where the lorry came from, since that was bound to be ascertained, sooner or later. But, of course, his yarn of having been on the road ever since he started from Plymouth was nonsense. It satisfied your friend Bleak, I have no doubt, but it doesn't satisfy us.

"We can very easily form a theory to explain what really happened. The problem was, how to dispose of the lorry once it had served its purpose. No doubt Figgis had noticed Bleak's place as he drove past during Wednesday night and decided that it would serve his purpose, being on the road, or one of the roads, from Plymouth to Blackdown. Speaking without the map, I should say that the distance from Blackdown to Whitchurch was between sixty and seventy miles.

"The business at the ventilating shaft was over, shall we say, by a quarter to six on Thursday evening. The car, which the lorry had ostensibly come to remove, was probably towed a short distance for appearances' sake. Then A and B changed places. B, who had driven the lorry from its temporary hiding-place to the shaft, took over the car and drove off to some destination unknown. A started in the lorry for Bleak's place, with something under three hours in which to cover the distance, which was plenty of time. Of course, he knew when the last train left Whitchurch, and was careful to arrive in time to catch it. And equally, of course, he made a detour so as to arrive at Bleak's place with his bonnet facing towards London. And you see now how useful he found those trade number plates. If Bleak had noticed and remembered the number, which was highly unlikely, they could only be traced back to Plymouth, and so would substantiate his story. He's a clever crook, there's no getting away from that."

"Too darn clever by half," Arnold grumbled. "The only thing for it that I can see is to circulate the best description I can, and hope for the best."

Merrion shook his head. "That would be very little use, I'm afraid. How do we know that the people in Wigland and Bunthorne's office, or the manager of the Celtic Garage, or Bleak, saw the real man? Their descriptions all seem to agree, certainly. But how do we know that they do not refer to another of A's disguises? Perhaps this pleasant-spoken, clean-shaven, smartly-dressed young man was created for the purpose and will never appear again."

Arnold grunted. "Hardly an optimist, are you?" he said. "Well, then, there's another way of trying to trace him. You said yourself that these chaps showed such an intimate knowledge of Sir Wilfred's habits that one of them must have been a member of his family or of his personal staff. I'm going to question each of them as to their movements on the Wednesday and Thursday."

"And I'm inclined to think that won't get you any further. I quite agree that one of them, A or B, must have been intimately connected with A or B. The other may have been a complete stranger. And I think it was A who was the stranger, acting under B's instructions.

"We know that B must have driven the lorry from its hiding-place to the shaft. We are agreed, I think, that the distance between these two points was inconsiderable. Since A drove the lorry to Bleak's, B must have taken charge of the car. What did he do with it? In all probability he took it to the spot which had served as the hiding-place of the lorry. All he had to do, then, was to cover this short distance twice. He was probably absent from his usual haunts for a couple of hours at most. And almost anybody can do that, without other people being a penny the wiser."

"Confound you!" Arnold exclaimed. "You throw cold water upon every suggestion I make. Suppose you try to be helpful for a change?"

"I'm only discouraging because I feel pretty sure that ordinary methods won't do in this case. We've got a pair of remarkably clever scoundrels to deal with, and they've left no loose threads behind them for us to catch hold of. But let's see if we can't worry out something about this hiding-place we've spoken of. We know, or rather, we have deduced, this much about it. It is within a radius of a dozen miles or so of the ventilating shaft, and it was capable of concealing a vehicle as conspicuous as a breakdown lorry for a whole day. I don't think, then, that it is likely to have been some secluded spot by the roadside, for instance. Or that it was in the open at all, for that matter. The risk of the lorry being seen, and questions asked, would have been too great. You see the point, don't you?"

"Yes, I see the point, all right," Arnold replied. "But I haven't the foggiest notion of what you're driving at."

"You'll understand in a moment. The next point in the argument is this. If the lorry was not left out in the open it must have been hidden somewhere safely under cover. In other words, it was put into a building of some kind, a shed or garage. Certainly not a public garage, or you would have heard of it by now. Besides, the risk of recognition would have been too great. Then a private building of some kind, to which only the conspirators had access. Does that suggest anything to you?"

"Only that since we don't know who the conspirators are, we can't tell what buildings they had access to."

"To what, as a rule, do people have sole access? Their own property. We are agreed that one of these two was intimate with Saxonby, and I have told you why I believe that this was B. Now, suppose that B lived somewhere near Blackdown? I've already explained why one of the conspirators most likely does so. Wouldn't his private garage be an ideal spot in which to hide the lorry? And B would have been operating from his house and usual haunts.

"Now, perhaps, you see the chance of a clue. You know where Mrs. Wardour and her husband live. But do you know where the other people who may be supposed to have been intimate with Saxonby live? You don't, because you have never thought it worth while to ask. But if I were you, my next step would be to make a list of addresses."

Arnold made no reply to this. But evidently he was revolving in his mind what Merrion had said. "Look here!" he exclaimed suddenly. "You said just now that A may have been a total stranger to Sir Wilfred. Yet A is the man who gave his name as Yates, and was admitted to Sir Wilfred's presence without question. How do you account for that?"

"Easily enough," Merrion replied. "Saxonby may have been expecting a messenger from a friend of his. He knew that the messenger would give the name of Yates, and he also knew the time that he would call. Consequently when the messenger arrived and was announced to him, he gave orders that he was to be sent up at once. It seems to me quite natural."

"Then it's the only natural thing I've come across in this case so far," Arnold growled. "Well, it's time I was getting along. I'll think over your suggestion of inquiring where all these people live. Good-night."

His departure left Merrion to his own thoughts. Arnold's last question had perplexed him more than he had cared to admit. The theory that Yates had been a messenger from a friend had occurred to him on the spur of the moment. But, on reflection, this theory seemed to raise two perplexing questions. Who was this friend, and why had he not been heard of since Saxonby's death? Merrion was still convinced that Yates had brought Saxonby something of value. If as the messenger of a friend of his, why had that friend not made some statement, since the valuable object had disappeared? That was the first question. The second concerned the name given by the messenger. Was it merely a coincidence that this was the same as that of Saxonby's lawyer?"

Dimly a suspicion began to form in Merrion's mind. It was ridiculous, of course. Sir Wilfred Saxonby had been a man of stainless reputation. A magistrate, against whom the only criticism that could be levelled was a certain severity of judgment. Chairman of Wigland and Bunthorne, an old-established firm with an established and honoured position in the City. During the whole course of the investigation no hint had been made in any way derogatory to Saxonby's character. And yet…

Without a shred of justification, Merrion's imagination persisted in its obstinate and contrary course. What if there had been a reverse to this picture of spotless respectability? What if Saxonby, unknown to his family, unknown to his staff, had indulged in some shady but doubtless profitable transaction, or series of transactions? If so, the visit of Yates, and its attendant circumstances, would become more explicable.

Merrion did not worry himself about the possible nature of these imaginary transactions. He assumed for the moment that they had existed. Obviously, Saxonby could not have appeared in them personally. He would have been compelled to employ a confidential agent. Yates had been that agent. The interview between them had been arranged for the purpose of giving the profits of the transaction to his principal. These profits, not necessarily in the form of money, formed the mysterious object X, of which Merrion had all along suspected the existence.

Fanciful though such a theory might be, it explained the two points which Arnold's question had raised. Yates became no longer the envoy from a friend, but Saxonby's accredited agent. No one but they knew of the existence of X, and consequently no one could remark upon its disappearance. Yates had been instructed by Saxonby himself to give that name at the office. Should the fact of his visit reach inquisitive ears, it would be assumed that Saxonby had merely received a visit from his lawyer, which would occasion no surprise.

Yates might conveniently be explained along those lines. But the very nature of their association would make it necessary for him to be segregated from Saxonby's ordinary and visible life. Yates could not have been intimate with his family or with the staff of Wigland and Bunthorne. Hence the necessity for B, who could provide the necessary information, and direct the conspiracy. Had Yates approached B in the first instance? It seemed highly improbable. Far more likely that B had in some way penetrated Saxonby's secret and determined to secure a share of the profits for himself.

If this had happened B had two courses open to him. He might have blackmailed Saxonby. But blackmail was always a dangerous game, and Saxonby, from all accounts, would hardly have been an easy person with which to play it. Or he might approach Yates and unfold to him a conspiracy to be carried through on a profit-sharing basis. No doubt he had adopted the latter course.

The more Merrion played with the idea, the better he liked it. It accounted satisfactorily for Saxonby's anxiety to have his son, his daughter and Torrance, out of the way at the time of Yates' visit. With the directors and the secretary of the firm out of London, Saxonby would be secure from observation. The junior staff would not concern themselves with any visitor whom he might have. It would never have done for Yates to have been seen by anybody in a position to ask questions. Something might have leaked out which would have given a clue to the secret.

Again, the five-pound notes took on a slightly more plausible aspect. If Yates had been Saxonby's agent, it was natural that the latter should supply him with money. He had cashed the cheque for that purpose. The notes had passed into the possession of Yates and had so formed part of the contents of the substituted wallet.

Yes, on the whole, Merrion found himself growing enamoured of his theory, in spite of the fact that he had no evidence with which to substantiate it. And, precisely because this evidence was altogether lacking, it would be better to say nothing to Arnold as yet. The inspector would reject it with the scorn it deserved. Later, if some clue could be discovered to the identity of B, it would be time enough.

XVI

INSPECTOR ARNOLD, IN SEEKING INFORMATION AS TO THE MEMbers of Sir Wilfred Saxonby's family, turned naturally to Torrance, the secretary of Wigland and Bunthorne. He might, of course, have approached Miss Olivia Saxonby. But, for one thing, he always found it easier to question a man than a woman, and, for another, he felt hardly conversant with the state of the Saxonby family politics. Mrs. Wardour had displayed no striking cousinly solicitude for Miss Olivia. It was at least possible that the latter might retaliate by supplying information with a definite bias to it.

So Arnold called once more at the serene and dignified offices in Shrubb Court and secured an interview with Torrance. He did not approach his object directly, but began by talking about Mr. Dredger, who was still prominently in his thoughts. As a business man, Torrance gave him a very high character. "The Manchester office has never been the same since he retired," he said. "He's a man who has a way with him, you know, and that always seemed to impress our customers. It impressed other people, too, and for that reason I'm personally not sorry that he's no longer an active member of the firm."

"I'm afraid I don't quite follow you there, Mr. Torrance," said Arnold.

"I wasn't being intentionally obscure. Between ourselves, some of us found old Dredger a bit of a nuisance. He is a regular toady, if ever there was one, and was always making up to the directors. That sort of thing didn't cut much ice with Sir Wilfred, and there were occasions when the two didn't exactly hit it off. But both Mr.

Richard and Mrs. Wardour fell for him, and in their eyes he could do nothing wrong. It used to make things in the office rather uncomfortable sometimes."

"Has he kept in touch with the directors since his retirement?"

"Oh, he looks in here occasionally. And when he was ill, Mrs. Wardour and Sir Richard and his wife were always going to Blackdown to see him. Mrs. Richard Saxonby in particular. They live quite close to Blackdown, between Westerham and Edenbridge."

The information which Arnold sought seemed to be coming of itself. He made no comment, but allowed Torrance to continue. "Old Dredger has a car, a little nine-horse Morstin, and he drives over to see the Saxonbys fairly often when they're at home, I believe. From one or two little things that have happened, I fancy he still tries to influence the affairs of the firm from outside. Now that Sir Wilfred is dead, I'm very much afraid that too much attention will be paid to his suggestions. And, between ourselves, if that turns out to be the case, I shall begin looking for another job."

"You don't agree with Mr. Dredger's suggestions, then?"

"They may be excellent," Torrance replied dryly, "but it would hardly be conducive to the smooth working of the office if it were suspected that the decisions of the directors were influenced by the opinions of the late Manchester manager. However, that's a personal matter with which I hardly need trouble you."

"I suppose that Mr. Richard Saxonby has a very nice place?"

"It's really a charming place, not very big, but with a very fine garden. Some people might think it a bit too isolated, for it stands by itself with trees all round it. The Saxonbys don't live there much in the winter; they've got a flat in Kensington. But in summer it is ideal. Of course they've both got cars. Mr. Richard has a Rolls-Royce, in which he drives up here, and Mrs. Richard a Morstin of the same vintage as old Dredger's."

"What becomes of the house when the Saxonbys are not there?" Arnold asked.

"Oh, it is shut up. The gardener lives in a cottage not far away, and he's about the place most of the day. And I believe old Dredger runs over sometimes to see that everything is all right."

Arnold took good care not to reveal his interest in this conversation. But he was not anxious to press Torrance too far, lest his curiosity should be aroused. He allowed him to wander off into other matters, and only, towards the end of his visit, secured a list of the addresses of all those who had been intimately connected with Sir Wilfred. For the most part they lived in London or its immediate suburbs, as, for instance, Torrance himself, who, it seemed, was married, had two children, and occupied a flat in Maida Vale. The only address situated anywhere near Blackdown was that of Sir Wilfred's son.

"I'm much obliged to you, Mr. Torrance," said Arnold as he closed his note-book. "By the way, you remember the visitor who called upon Sir Wilfred here on Thursday afternoon. He gave his name as Yates, you told me. Isn't that the name of the solicitor whom Sir Wilfred employed in his private affairs?"

"Yes, it is, as I have learnt since. Mrs. Wardour told me. If I knew it before, I had forgotten it. You must understand that though I was entirely in Sir Wilfred's confidence as regards the affairs of the firm, it was only on exceptional occasions that he spoke to me of his private affairs. That explains the visit, of course."

"I'm not sure that it does," Arnold replied. "Mr. Yates, the lawyer, assures me that neither he nor his son visited Sir Wilfred that day, or, for that matter, communicated with him in any way."

"That sounds queer," said Torrance. "Who can the chap have been, I wonder?"

"I'd very much like to find out. But I mustn't waste any more of your time, Mr. Torrance. Good-morning."

Arnold went back to the Yard and got into touch with Merrion. That same afternoon they took a car and set out to find Richard Saxonby's house.

This they accomplished, but not without some little difficulty. The place was certainly remote, lying well off the main road. A few scattered cottages surrounded it, but from none of these was the house visible. At last they discovered the entrance gate, from which a short drive led to a small picturesque house standing in a beautifully-kept garden. The windows were shuttered and there was no sign of life to be seen.

"Half a minute, before we look for that gardener you talk about," said Merrion, pulling a map from his pocket and spreading it out. "Here we are and there's the ventilating shaft of Blackdown Tunnel. Four and a half miles as the crow flies, and say six or seven by road. That fits in very nicely with my theory. Now let's walk round and see what we can find."

They had not gone very far when the gardener, attracted by the sound of the car, appeared. He was an intelligent, middle-aged man, and gave his name as Quince. He had been in Mr. Richard Saxonby's service ever since he had bought the house, and that was many years back.

Arnold began his interrogation. "Now, Quince, do you remember Thursday of last week?" he asked.

"I remember it well enough, sir," Quince replied readily. "It was the day I went to Norwich about those rhododendrons."

"You went to Norwich that day? A longish journey from here, surely! Do you often go as far afield as that?"

"Not very often, sir. It was the first time that I'd been further than London for the past ten years and more. But orders are orders, and that's what Mrs. Wardour said. So I went and gave the order, and I hope the master and mistress will be pleased with what I chose."

"Mrs. Wardour?" exclaimed Arnold. "Where does she come in? Let's have the whole story, Quince?"

"Why, you see, sir, it was like this. When I got back home on the Wednesday, having done my day's work, there was a letter for me that the missus told me had come by the afternoon post. I opened it and found it was from Mrs. Wardour. But there, perhaps you'd like to see it for yourself, sir. I've got it in my pocket still."

He produced an envelope, rather grimy from contact with earthy fingers, and handed it to the inspector, who looked at it carefully. The address was typewritten and the envelope bore a London postmark, 12.30 a.m., November 13th. It had therefore been posted late on Tuesday evening.

Inside the envelope was a letter typed upon the headed paper of Wigland and Bunthorne. The contents of the letter were as follows:

> "Dear Quince,—I have had a letter from my brother who, as you know, is in America. He has decided to fill the bed opposite the front door with rhododendrons, and wants this done at once, before it is too late to put the plants in. He wants you to go to Norwich and see Fremlins, the nurserymen there, as he has been told theirs are the best. Tell them how many you want, and choose the best varieties. They can send the bill in to my brother at the Kensington address, and he will pay it as soon as he returns. You had better go on Thursday, without fail. I enclose two pounds to cover your expenses. Yours sincerely,
>
> "Irene Wardour."

The signature was written in ink, in an obviously feminine hand.

Arnold passed this letter on to Merrion. "So you went to Norwich on Thursday, did you, Quince?" he said. "You started pretty early, I expect?"

"Yes, and got back late, sir. I didn't manage to come to work here at all that day. Still, there's no harm done. There's not a lot one can be doing in the garden at this time of year."

"Were you surprised to get this letter?"

"Surprised, sir? No, why would I be? I know Mrs. Wardour well enough, she often comes over here when the master and mistress are at home, and she's very fond of flowers. And the master often talked about putting rhododendrons in that bed. He thought they'd make a fine show from the front windows when they were in bloom."

"I dare say they would," said Arnold absently. "If you hadn't received that letter, you'd have been up here at work on Thursday?"

"Yes, sir. I come up every day and do my work. And most Sunday afternoons I and the missus take a stroll round. That's when the house is empty, of course. I live in the first cottage down the road, the one with the roses in front of it. It's the best part of a mile from here, but I've got my bike, and it don't take me long to slip backwards and forwards."

"You know Mr. Dredger, of course. Have you seen him lately?"

"He was over here in his car the Wednesday afore I went to Norwich, sir. He passed the time of day with me, and I gave him a few handfuls of sprouts. They're rotting on the plants, now that the master and mistress are in America. When they're in London I send them up vegetables twice a week, regular. And the master will drive down sometimes and fetch them himself."

"Did Mr. Dredger stay here long on Wednesday?"

"Not more than a few minutes, sir. He asked me to unlock the house for him—I've got the back door key, you understand, sir. I let him in, and I suppose he had a walk round, just to see that everything was all right, like he often does. And then I went down to the far end of the garden, and when I came back he'd gone."

"There is a garage here, I suppose?"

"Yes, sir, a big one, that the master had built when he bought the house. It's round at the back, if you'd care to see it."

"Yes, I think we may as well have a look at it," Arnold replied. "Don't you, Merrion?"

Merrion nodded. "I think it might prove interesting," he said.

"Then perhaps you'll come this way, gentlemen," said Quince. "I'll have to get the key. It hangs on a nail just inside the back door."

They followed him round the house, and taking a key from his pocket, he unlocked the door and walked in. Arnold and Merrion waited outside. They could hear Quince grumbling to himself and then he reappeared. "The key's not where it ought to be," he said. "I can't make it out. I haven't used it for a fortnight or more. Surely I can't have gone and left it in the lock all that while?"

Arnold glanced significantly at Merrion. "We'd better go and see," he said. The garage was only a few paces distant, a new brick building with two pairs of stout doors. But there was no key in either of the locks. "Can't make it out," Quince repeated. "But if you gentlemen want to see inside the garage I'll soon manage that."

He pointed to a sash window in the side wall. "The fastener's broken," he continued. "It won't take me long to get my knife under the bottom window and prise it up." He suited the action to the word and opened the window without difficulty. Then he climbed through it and opened one pair of double doors from inside.

The interior of the garage, thus revealed, was big enough to accommodate two large cars. But it contained only one small one, a nine-horse-power Morstin saloon. Though perhaps a shade more carefully kept, it resembled Dredger's car in every particular. It was of similar age and colour, and it was fitted with a fairly new set of Dunlop tyres.

"Whose car is this?" Arnold asked.

"It belongs to the mistress, sir. She always leaves it here for the winter, for she doesn't like driving in London, I've heard her say."

"I don't wonder at that," Merrion remarked. "Driving in London is not much fun now, what with traffic lights and Belisha beacons and other modern means of obstruction." He walked up to the car, inspected it critically, took off the cap of the radiator and glanced within. "H'm, if I were going to leave a car in an unheated garage all the winter, I should run off the water," he said quietly.

"Why, sir, that's just what the mistress told me to do, last thing before she went away. I turned on the tap at the bottom and ran off the water into a bucket."

"You're perfectly sure you did so, and not only intended to do it?"

"Certain, sir. And the master could bear me out if he was here. He was in the garage at the time and saw me do it."

"Well, the radiator is full now. Come and have a look, Arnold."

The inspector satisfied himself on this point, then continued his questioning. "Do Mr. and Mrs. Saxonby keep a chauffeur?" he asked.

"No, sir. They look after the cars themselves. And when they want washing, I do the job, or if I'm too busy, a chap that lives down the road comes up."

"Mr. Saxonby owns a Rolls-Royce, I understand. Where is that car now?"

"He drove it up to the makers for overhaul, sir, just before he left."

"Then only Mrs. Saxonby's car has been in the garage since then?"

"That's right, sir. And that was at the latter end of September."

"That's interesting," said Merrion. "You're accustomed to washing the cars, you say, Quince. Do you ever wash out the garage?"

"Once a week when the master and mistress are at home, sir. And when they go away I give it a good scrub out after they've gone, and leave it until just before they come back."

"When did you last scrub out the garage?"

"The day after the master and mistress went to America, sir."

"And no other car but this one has been in here since, you say. Then how do you account for this?"

He pointed to the concrete floor. In the centre of the vacant half of the garage were several spots of black, sticky oil, still semi-liquid.

Quince looked at these with an expression of almost ludicrous amazement. "Now, where can they have come from?" he demanded. "They weren't there when I was last in here, that I'll swear."

"And when was that?"

"Last time I used the key, sir. About a fortnight back, but I can't mind the day exactly."

"Before your journey to Norwich?"

"Oh, yes, sir, before that. Friday or Saturday of the week before, it must have been. I don't have occasion to come in here much in the winter."

"That oil dripped from the gear-box of a car," said Merrion decisively. "Now, let's get back to the missing key. You used it to get in here about a fortnight ago. When you locked up the garage you hung the key in the usual place, I suppose?"

"Well, sir, I could have sworn I did. But, seeing that it isn't there now..."

"Could anybody have taken it, since then?"

"Not unless they got into the house, and I don't see how they could have done that. Nobody else but me has a key, and I always keep the door locked when I'm not about. Besides, there's nobody comes up here at this time of year."

"You said that Mr. Dredger was here on Wednesday, last week," said Arnold sharply.

"Oh, yes, sir, Mr. Dredger. But he's a friend of the family. I wasn't counting him."

"And on that occasion he asked you to let him into the house?"

"That's right, sir. But Mr. Dredger can't never have taken the key. What would he take it into his head to do a thing like that for?"

"People do unaccountable things sometimes," Arnold replied. "Now, look here, Quince. You were not up here at all on the Thursday you went to Norwich. Suppose somebody had stolen the key of the garage. Would it have been possible for anybody to drive a car here early in the morning, leave it in the garage all day, and drive it away again in the evening without anybody knowing anything about it?"

"Well, sir, I suppose they might have done. Especially if they came from Medbridge way, up the lane. There aren't no houses along that for nigh on a mile. But what would make them do it?"

Arnold made no reply to this. He and Merrion devoted themselves to a minute examination of the garage and of Mrs. Saxonby's car without finding anything to reward their efforts. They then asked Quince to show them the interior of the house. This also they searched thoroughly, still without success. This done, they re-entered the car which had brought them and started to drive back to London. "Well, and what about Dredger now?" was Arnold's first question. "Are you still going to maintain that he had nothing to do with it?"

"I don't know," replied Merrion doubtfully. "My faith in his complete innocence is a bit shaken, I confess. That missing key is infernally suggestive. What's your theory now?"

"That Dredger was the man whom we've agreed to call B," replied Arnold promptly.

"Then you've got to admit that somebody disguised himself as Dredger, at least in the evening. If Dredger was B, he was working things at the top of the ventilating shaft at the time when somebody exactly like him was travelling in the five o'clock train. And why, in heaven's name, should a criminal disguise himself as his accomplice? If Dredger had been involved it would have been in the interests of the gang to keep him from suspicion as far as possible. Certainly not to run any chance of putting the police on his track. No, I'm pretty sure Dredger wasn't B."

"He fulfils all the conditions which you yourself laid down," Arnold replied doggedly. "He was intimate with Sir Wilfred's family, he knew all about the affairs of the firm, and he lives close to the shaft."

"That's just why he was such a suitable man to impersonate. And there's another reason. He was in the habit of driving over to the Saxonby's place now and then. Anybody looking like him, and driving Mrs. Saxonby's car, which you say is exactly similar to his, would attract no attention, even if he were actually seen on the premises. He would be taken for Dredger, paying one of his periodical visits. Gosh! This is a tangle! Let's see if we can straighten it out a bit.

"Yates, or Figgis, or whatever he chooses to call himself, drove the breakdown lorry from Plymouth. Early on Thursday morning he reached the Saxonby's place, and put the lorry in their garage. Those spots of oil on the floor tell their own story. But in order to do this he had to have the key of the garage which, in any case, we know to have disappeared. We'll suppose for the moment that Dredger conveyed it to him, though I don't quite see how."

"Dredger took the key and left it in some prearranged spot on the premises. Under a stone in the yard, for instance."

"Yes, that will do. Next, Quince had to be got out of the way during the whole of Thursday. Most providentially, Quince receives a letter from Mrs. Wardour, sending him on an errand to Norwich. It's really remarkable."

"I shall see Mrs. Wardour and ask her about that letter," said Arnold.

"I should. One point in particular seems to me to want a bit of explaining. Mrs. Wardour is supposed to have been in the South of

France during the whole of last week. How then did she come to post a letter in London late on Tuesday evening?"

Arnold groaned. "Are you suggesting that she was in the plot, too?"

"I wouldn't go so far as that until I had definite proof that she wrote the letter. By the way, there's a point about that letter not to be lost sight of. We have it from Quince that Richard Saxonby had spoken about putting rhododendrons in that particular bed. Mrs. Wardour might well have known this. If she can prove that she didn't write the letter you'll have to look for some one else who also knew about the rhododendrons.

"But let's get back to the sequence of events on Thursday. Yates drove the lorry into the Saxonby's garage. Later in the morning, disguised as Dredger—no, don't interrupt, I'm as much entitled to my theory as you are to yours—later in the morning, I say, Yates drove Mrs. Saxonby's car to the shaft and left it there. He then went up to London, and we know what he did there. In the evening B arrives at the garage. He takes out the lorry and drives it to the shaft. A, having been fished out of the tunnel, takes over the lorry and fetches up eventually at Bleak's place near Whitchurch. B takes Mrs. Saxonby's car and returns it to its accustomed place in her garage. And then, confound him, he disappears into thin air, so far as we are concerned. I say, I wonder if Richard Saxonby is really in America all this time?"

"Why should Richard Saxonby conspire with Yates to murder his father?"

"Because, perhaps, his father was up to profitable mischief of some kind. Don't, for heaven's sake, let's get on to the subject of motive at this stage. Find out who wrote that letter to Quince. It may have been Mrs. Wardour, but I don't believe it was. B wrote that letter, I'm convinced. It's just possible that Mrs. Wardour may have been B, I suppose. But if she was, would she have signed the letter in her own name?"

"Quince would hardly have obeyed the instructions of anybody else, I should imagine."

"Probably not. But his very obedience causes a complication. As soon as his master comes back, or at all events as soon as he sees Quince, he will hear about those rhododendrons. And then, unless I am greatly mistaken, it will come out that he never wrote to his sister at all, or if he did, that he never gave her the message for Quince. If Mrs. Wardour wrote the letter, how did she propose to explain all that? It seems to me far more likely that Richard Saxonby wrote it. In which case no need for explanations would arise."

"Richard Saxonby is supposed to arrive in England to-morrow," said Arnold thoughtfully. "I shall make it my business to meet him. Meanwhile, as soon as we get back to London, I shall call on Mrs. Wardour. She may have something interesting to tell me about those confounded rhododendrons."

XVII

ARNOLD WAS ONCE MORE FORTUNATE IN FINDING IRENE Wardour at home. He opened the conversation by inquiring about Richard Saxonby. "You are expecting your brother home to-morrow, are you not, Mrs. Wardour?" he asked.

"I am going down to Southampton to meet him," she replied. "He is on the *Iberia*, and she is due there at two o'clock in the afternoon."

"Do you happen to know when the *Iberia* left New York?"

"Last Friday, a week ago to-day. She was the first boat to sail after he received Olivia's cable telling him of my father's death."

"Have you heard from your brother since he was in America, Mrs. Wardour?"

"I've had a couple of letters from him. Nothing of any importance."

"Did he, by chance, mention the subject of rhododendrons in either of them?"

Mrs. Wardour looked at the inspector as though she suspected him of being under the influence of drink. "Rhododendrons!" she exclaimed. "No, certainly not! Why in the world should he write to me about rhododendrons?"

"Perhaps, Mrs. Wardour, because you knew that he intended to plant rhododendrons in the bed opposite his front door."

"I haven't the remotest notion of what you are talking about," she replied sharply. "Now you mention it, I remember Richard saying something of the kind one day last summer. But I had completely forgotten it until this moment. I'm not particularly interested in gardening myself."

"But you have heard of Fremlins, the nurserymen, of Norwich?"

"I have heard of them, but only in connection with the business of Wigland and Bunthorne. We occasionally import rare shrubs and plants for them."

This accounted for a fact which had puzzled Arnold. Fremlins might have had their doubts about executing an order given by a strange gardener, unsupported by any sort of reference. But Richard Saxonby's name would be familiar to them, and Quince's visit would have occasioned them no surprise. Perhaps this might give an additional clue to the identity of the writer of the letter.

The inspector drew from his pocket the letter itself, so folded that only the signature was visible, and showed it thus to Mrs. Wardour. "Do you recognise this signature?" he asked.

"Certainly," she replied, with hardly more than a glance at it. "It is mine."

"You are sure of that?"

"As sure of it as I am that you are asking me questions of which I don't in the least understand the drift."

Arnold unfolded the letter and held it out to her. "Perhaps if you will read that it will enable you to understand," he said.

Mrs. Wardour read the letter, with ever-growing astonishment.

"I don't understand it at all!" she exclaimed. "I certainly never wrote that letter. Nor, as I told you before, has Richard so much as mentioned rhododendrons in writing to me from America. This must be a joke, though I don't quite see the point of it. Somebody seems to have been pulling Quince's leg."

"I should very much like to know who that somebody was, Mrs. Wardour," said Arnold sternly. "You admit that the signature of the letter is yours?"

"Yes, it is certainly mine. I think, though, that I can account for that. Before I went abroad I went down to Mavis Court to spend a day with my father. While I was there he asked me to sign my name on half a dozen sheets of the firm's notepaper. It sometimes happens that our letters require the signature of two directors. As both Richard and I would be away for the next week or two, my father wished to have my signature, to which he could add his own, in case of necessity."

"Do you know what became of those sheets of paper, Mrs. Wardour?"

"My father put them away in his desk," she replied. And then, as an afterthought, she added: "Olivia was in the room at the time. And I see that the day on which Quince was told to go to Norwich was the day on which my father was shot."

"Yes, that is so," Arnold agreed in a tone which suggested that the coincidence had struck him for the first time. "But if you did not write this letter I am bound to inquire who did. By the way, do you happen to remember where you were on Tuesday evening of last week?"

"Tuesday evening? Yes, that was the day before my husband left me and came home. We were at Cannes, and we spent the evening with some friends at their hotel."

"Thank you, Mrs. Wardour. Now, can you offer any suggestions as to who might have written this letter?"

"Olivia saw me sign the sheets of paper, and she saw my father put them away. Besides, she's got a typewriter, I know. She fancies that she's got a gift for writing short stories, but people don't seem to appreciate her gift."

"Would Miss Saxonby be likely to know the name of your brother's gardener, that the question of putting rhododendrons in that particular bed had been discussed, and that your firm had had dealings with Fremlins?"

"I don't see why she shouldn't have known. She might have heard all those things from my father, or from one of us."

"Do you happen to know if Mr. Dredger is fond of gardening?"

"Yes, he is. He and Richard can talk of nothing else sometimes."

"Perhaps your brother discussed the planting of that bed with him. And he would, of course, have known of your firm's business relations with Fremlins?"

"Yes, I suppose he would. But he isn't at all the sort of person to write a letter like that. He would never dream of doing anything that might annoy Richard or myself. Besides, how could he have got hold of that sheet of paper with my signature on it?"

This was, for the present at least, unanswerable. Arnold left Mrs. Wardour and returned to Scotland Yard more puzzled than ever. His conversation with her had convinced him that she had told the truth. And her explanation of the appearance of her signature upon it was probably the correct one.

What was Sir Wilfred most likely to have done with the signed sheets of paper? He was hardly likely to have kept them at Mavis Court, where they would be of little use to him. He had probably taken them up to the office on his next visit. Torrance might know something about them. Arnold set out to find out.

But Torrance could tell him very little. "I know that Mrs. Wardour signed some sheets of paper in blank before she went abroad, because she told me so," he said. "But what Sir Wilfred did with them I can't say. None of them were used, since no occasion arose for doing so. And I don't think that Sir Wilfred can have brought them here. If he had he would have given them to me to put in the safe, or he would have locked them away in his room. He didn't give them to me, and they are certainly not in his room now, for Mrs. Wardour and I went through everything there only yesterday."

"How many typewriters have you in the office, Mr. Torrance?"

"Fourteen all told. They are all the same make, Remingwoods."

"Could you let me have samples of work done by each of them?"

"Easily enough. If you'll wait a minute or two I'll have it done."

Torrance disappeared and came back shortly with fourteen slips of paper, on each of which had been typed the phrase: "The quick brown fox jumps over the lazy dog." "Not a very enlightening statement, I'm afraid," he said. "But you'll observe that apparently meaningless sentence brings in all the letters of the alphabet."

"Thanks," Arnold replied. "That's just what I wanted." He took out the letter and compared it with each of the specimens in turn. Even to the uneducated eye it was apparent that it bore no similarity to any of them. Then he handed the letter to Torrance. "Read that and tell me what you think of it," he said.

Torrance read it without any great interest. "I don't see anything peculiar about it," he said. "Mrs. Wardour transmits her brother's orders to his gardener. Why not?"

"Mrs. Wardour assures me that she did not write the letter."

"Then it is a bit queer, I'll admit. I'm beginning to understand what you're after. And perhaps I might be able to give you a hint. I know something about typewriters. That letter was typed with a Regal portable, and not a particularly new one, either. We haven't got such a thing on the place. Nor has Mrs. Wardour, I'm pretty sure."

"Do you know anybody who has?"

"Oh, there are plenty of them about. Let me think, now. Yes, I do know of somebody who uses one. Excuse me a minute, will you?"

He disappeared for the second time and returned with a sheet of paper on which a few words were typed. "I hereby acknowledge the receipt of £125 (one hundred and twenty-five pounds) from Messrs. Wigland and Bunthorne Ltd." A twopenny stamp was affixed, and over this was written the signature "Malcolm Dredger," and the date.

"Receipt for his last quarter's pension," said Torrance. "That was typed with the Regal portable which he always uses."

The type of the receipt exactly resembled that of the letter. But Arnold remembered Mrs. Wardour's question. He repeated it to Torrance. "Anything that we say to one another is strictly confidential, you understand that. Can you suggest any way in which Mr. Dredger could have obtained a sheet of the firm's notepaper with Mrs. Wardour's signature on it?"

Torrance frowned. "I somehow can't imagine old Dredger playing a trick like that," he replied. "But I suppose, since you ask me, that he could easily find a way of getting hold of Mrs. Wardour's signature if he had wanted it. It doesn't follow that that letter was typed upon one of the sheets signed by her before she went abroad, does it?"

Arnold went back to Scotland Yard, more firmly convinced than ever that Dredger had been concerned in the plot to murder Sir Wilfred. He sent the letter, and the receipt, which he had borrowed from Torrance, to the appropriate department for expert examination. Then, once more, he turned to the baffling question of the identity of the person known as B. Merrion had suggested Richard Saxonby. That could be settled, one way or the other, next day. If Richard Saxonby disembarked from the *Iberia* on her arrival at Southampton he could not have been in the neighbourhood of Blackdown on the Thursday, since the *Iberia* had left New York on the following day.

Then, with Dredger still at the back of his mind, the inspector began to look at the matter in a fresh light. He agreed with Merrion that one of the conspirators must have possessed an amazing fund of special knowledge. Every fresh discovery emphasised that fact. But was it necessary that this individual should have been either A or B? Might they not have carried out the crime upon information supplied by some third person? If so, that person had undoubtedly been Dredger.

Arnold's meditations were interrupted by the entrance of the expert to whom he had confided the letter and the receipt. "We can't actually swear that these two documents were typed with the same machine," he said. "It's impossible to do that unless there is some peculiarity in one of the letters, and in this case there isn't. On the other hand, the probability is that they were. But not, I think, by the same person. The receipt shows a distinctly heavy touch, while the letter shows just the reverse. And you'll find that the touch of a person accustomed to typing varies very little. I would hazard a guess that the fingers which typed the receipt were older than those which typed the letter."

Left alone once more, Arnold considered this fresh piece of evidence. He had the greatest respect for Merrion's judgment. He would readily have admitted that more than once, in previous cases upon which he had been consulted, his friend's imaginative theories had been justified. But, in the present instance, his insistence upon Dredger's innocence seemed to be contradicted by every fresh fact which came to light.

In the expert's opinion, the letter to Quince had been typed, if not by Dredger, at least upon his machine. Dredger, then, had supplied the information, and either A or B had typed the letter. The inspector felt that the circumstantial evidence against Dredger was more than sufficient to justify his arrest. And perhaps, once he was in the hands of the police, he could be induced to reveal the identity of his confederates.

Arnold was wondering whether he should put the matter to his chief, for his decision, when he received a summons to the Assistant Commissioner's room. He found there two elderly men, both looking very anxious and perturbed, to whom the Assistant Commissioner introduced him.

"This is Inspector Arnold, who has been investigating certain circumstances connected with the death of Sir Wilfred Saxonby. Now, gentlemen, if you will tell us your story in full, the inspector and I will do our best to help you."

The two men glanced at one another, and the elder spoke. "In order that you may understand the sequence of events, I had better tell my version first. My name is Harrison, and I am the manager of the Bank of Great Britain, in Lombard Street. My friend here is Mr. Cecil Kirby, one of our most esteemed customers.

"During the morning of Tuesday, November 12th, a man called at the bank. He said that he carried a letter of introduction from Messrs. Wigland and Bunthorne, and asked to see me. I should explain that this firm are among our customers, and that we also held the private account of Sir Wilfred Saxonby. The caller, who gave the name of Malcolm Dredger, was shown into my office."

Arnold started at the familiar name. "Can you describe him, Mr. Harrison?" he asked.

"He appeared to be between sixty and seventy, and had a short grey beard and rather a prominent nose. He gave me the letter, which I shall be pleased to hand over to you. It was written on the usual notepaper of Wigland and Bunthorne, and was signed by the chairman, the late Sir Wilfred Saxonby, and also by one of the directors, Mrs. Irene Wardour.

"The letter explained that until recently Mr. Dredger had been managing the Manchester office of the firm, and that he possessed their implicit confidence. They, and certain other individuals whose names were not specified, had decided to employ him as their intermediary in certain transactions involving the import of foreign produce. For that purpose they wished an account to be opened with us in Mr. Dredger's name. Cheques on this account were only to be honoured when signed by both Mr. Dredger and Sir Wilfred Saxonby.

"Those are the essential points of the letter, which appeared then, and to my mind still appears, perfectly genuine. Mr. Dredger wrote a specimen of his signature in my presence. He then produced two cheques, endorsed with that signature, which he asked should be paid into the account. Each of these cheques was for twenty-five thousand pounds, and were payable to Malcolm Dredger. One was drawn upon the private account of Sir Wilfred Saxonby. The other was drawn upon the account of Mr. Cecil Kirby. Mr. Kirby, as I knew, had left for a tour in Northern Europe on the previous Saturday, and the cheque bore that date, November 9th. I accepted these cheques, and gave Mr. Dredger a cheque-book. After some general conversation, he left my office.

"He appeared again at the bank just after it had opened on Friday, November 15th. He then presented a cheque on his account, bearing the signatures of himself and Sir Wilfred Saxonby. This cheque was for £48,973, and he explained that he required that sum with which to purchase foreign currency, which was to be forwarded to Kirby. This cheque was paid, in notes. I have here a list of their numbers. It was not until an hour or so later that I was informed, by Mr. Torrance, the secretary of Messrs. Wigland and Bunthorne, of Sir Wilfred Saxonby's death."

Mr. Harrison glanced at his companion, who nodded. "I will take up the story here," said the latter. "I have considerable interests in Northern Europe, and I had known Saxonby, both personally and in the way of business, for many years before his death. Unfortunately, some ten years ago, a most unfortunate affair interrupted our friendship. I need not trouble you with the details. We disagreed over the terms of a mutual agreement, and the matter went to arbitration. The decision was given in my favour, and Saxonby appeared to think that I had tricked him in some way. For a long time he refused to speak to me, but about last Christmas he wrote to me, admitting that his attitude had been unreasonable, and asking me to overlook it. We arranged a meeting at which a complete reconciliation took place. Since then we have usually lunched together on the days when he was in the City.

"More than once, on these occasions, he dropped hints of a scheme which he was maturing. He excused himself from being more explicit on the grounds that he had not yet fully thought out all the details. He gave me to understand, however, that it involved our co-operation, through an intermediary, in the importation of food-stuffs. I told him that as soon as he was ready to put up a definite proposition I would give it the most favourable consideration. This was the position when I went abroad on November 9th."

Here Mr. Harrison intervened. "Not long previous to that date, Sir Wilfred Saxonby came to see me at the bank. When we had completed our business he told me that he had every prospect of interesting Mr. Kirby in a scheme which would prove profitable to them both. It was owing to this remark that I was not surprised when Dredger presented cheques from Sir Wilfred and Mr. Kirby for similar amounts."

"I returned to London yesterday evening," Kirby continued. "On reaching home my wife told me that during my absence, on the Monday after my departure, burglars had entered our house during dinner. Her dressing-room had been searched, presumably for jewellery, but though various objects had been displaced, nothing had been taken. She had reported the matter to the police. It was not until later in the evening that I discovered that a desk in my study had been broken open and its contents had been disturbed. The only thing which had been taken was my cheque-book. I had not taken this abroad with me, since I was using traveller's cheques. This morning I called upon Mr. Harrison, who mentioned the cheque said to have been drawn by me in favour of Malcolm Dredger. I assured him that I had drawn no such cheque, and that it must therefore be a forgery. He showed me the cheque, and I am bound to admit that the signature would have deceived even myself. The cheque itself had been taken from the book stolen from my desk."

Mr. Harrison produced an envelope, which he laid on Sir Edric Conway's table. "That contains the three cheques in question," he said. "With them are genuine cheques drawn by Sir Wilfred and Mr. Kirby, for purposes of comparison. You will also find the letter of introduction from Messrs. Wigland and Bunthorne, and the numbers of the notes issued to Malcolm Dredger, who, apart from being a consummate rogue, appears to have been a very capable forger. I need hardly say how fervently I hope that you may be able to trace him."

"There won't be any difficulty about that," Arnold replied, in a tone of triumph which he made no attempt to conceal. "We know where to lay our hands on Dredger. In fact, he is at this very moment under the observation of the police."

XVIII

THE ARREST OF DREDGER FOLLOWED AS A MATTER OF COURSE. Immediately upon the conclusion of the interview Arnold went to Blackdown and saw the local police. Dredger, loudly protesting his innocence, was taken into custody.

Meanwhile the documents supplied by Mr. Harrison were submitted to the handwriting experts, with a request for report as soon as possible. Arnold received this that same evening, and, having read it through, rang up Merrion and asked him to come to the Yard. On his arrival he told him of the forgery and the steps which had been taken. Finally he gave him the report. "Now see if you can make head or tail of that," he said. "For I confess I can't."

The report was as follows:

> 1. The cheque drawn by Cecil Kirby in favour of Malcolm Dredger. This has been compared with genuine cheques drawn by Mr. Kirby, and with a receipt signed by Malcolm Dredger. (This was the receipt given to Arnold by Mr. Torrance.) The conclusions arrived at are as follows:
>
> The body of the cheque, that is the name of the payee and the amount, is in a disguised handwriting closely resembling Mr. Kirby's but distinguishable from it by certain peculiarities.
>
> The signature is an excellent imitation of Mr. Kirby's. It must have been written by some person who was familiar with the type of pen and the ink habitually used by him. But we have no hesitation in declaring the signature to be a forgery.
>
> The endorsement, though it bears some resemblance to the

signature of Malcolm Dredger on the receipt, is, in essentials, a very poor imitation of it. The endorsement is undoubtedly forged. It, however, exactly resembles the signature "Malcolm Dredger" contained in the specimen signature supplied by the bank.

There is reason to believe that the body of the cheque, the signature and the endorsement were written by the same person at the same time. This person, for convenience, may be referred to as the forger.

2. The cheque drawn by Wilfred Saxonby in favour of Malcolm Dredger. This has been compared with genuine cheques drawn by Sir Wilfred, with the cheque numbered 1, and with the receipt previously mentioned. The conclusions are as follows:

The body of the cheque is in a disguised handwriting, resembling, but easily distinguishable from, that of Sir Wilfred. It was almost certainly written by the same person on the body of cheque 1. This makes it probable that only one forger is implicated. But the resemblance of the false to the real is not so close in cheque 2 as in cheque 1.

The signature of the cheque is undoubtedly genuine. By no test has it been possible to discover any disparity between it and Sir Wilfred's usual signature.

The endorsement is exactly similar to that of cheque 1 and to the specimen. It is certainly the work of the forger.

There is reason to believe that the body of the cheque and the endorsement were written by the forger at the same time. The signature appears to have been written some time previously.

3. The cheque drawn by Wilfred Saxonby and Malcolm Dredger in favour of Malcolm Dredger. This has been compared with

cheques 1 and 2, and with the specimen signature. The conclusions are as follows:

The body of the cheque was written by the forger in the handwriting of the alleged Malcolm Dredger. It bears some resemblance to specimens of the handwriting of the real Malcolm Dredger, supplied by Messrs. Wigland and Bunthorne. But the disparity between the false and the true can easily be demonstrated.

The signature "Wilfred Saxonby" is undoubtedly genuine. But it was written a day or two before the body of the cheque and the second signature. The latter is the work of the forger, and is exactly similar to the endorsements on cheques 1 and 2.

The endorsement is also the work of the forger, similar in every respect to his other copies of Malcolm Dredger's handwriting. But it was written after the body of the cheque and the second signature, and blotting-paper was applied to it as soon as written.

4. The letter of introduction. The only written portions of this are the signatures. That of Wilfred Saxonby is undoubtedly genuine. That of Irene Wardour has been compared with the signature on a letter supplied by Inspector Arnold. (This was the letter to Quince.) In this case also there is no doubt of the genuineness of the signature.

"Well, what do you make of it?" asked Arnold, when Merrion had completed his perusal of the report.

"I shouldn't like to answer that question offhand," replied Merrion diplomatically. "If your people are right, as I expect they are, that report suggests the most amazing conspiracy I ever heard of. And a devilishly ingenious one, too. For the moment, if you don't mind my saying so, the most obvious thing about it is that it lets out the unhappy Dredger."

"On the charge of forgery, perhaps," said Arnold grimly. "But now that I've got him safely under lock and key, I'm going to keep him there. I've found out a bit more since I saw you last. That letter to Quince was typed on a machine belonging to him. What about that?"

"That may turn out a valuable clue, though perhaps not quite in the way you expect. But what's your theory about this forgery?"

"It was carried out by somebody who had been spying on Sir Wilfred and Kirby. That's plain enough. He had overheard Sir Wilfred's suggestion of co-operation, and decided to use this for his own ends. Somebody who had access to cheques signed in blank by Sir Wilfred. Since he only came up to town occasionally, I expect he left a supply of blank signed cheques with his cashier. That accounts for his being the only genuine signature among the lot."

"Possibly. But what about cheque 3? How did he come to sign a cheque that wasn't his?"

"That puzzled me for a bit, but I've got it now. His signature was the first thing to be written upon it. Now look at these cheques, they came back from the experts with the report. 2 is out of Sir Wilfred's own book, 3 is out of the book supplied by the bank to the forger. But they are exactly similar, except for the printed serial number. If this cheque number 3 had been slipped in among others from Sir Wilfred's book, and given to him to sign, he would never have noticed that the numbers did not run concurrently."

Merrion smiled. "Ingenious," he said. "But I'm not quite sure that that is exactly what happened. And what about the signatures on the letter of introduction, which are also genuine?"

"That letter is written on one of half a dozen sheets of paper signed by Mrs. Wardour. I'll tell you about that later. Sir Wilfred was induced to add his signature to hers before the letter was written."

"He seems to have been a person of a trusting disposition. I wish I could share your opinion that it will turn out to be as simple as all that. What bearing do you suppose this forgery has upon Sir Wilfred's death?"

"A fairly obvious one, it seems to me. Sir Wilfred was murdered to give the forger time to get clear away. Kirby was abroad and would not be back for some days after cheque 3 was cashed. But Sir Wilfred might discover the fraud at any moment. He might call at the bank, or Harrison might communicate with him. As it is, his death means that the forger has eight days' start of us."

"So that the forger was also a murderer? He was, in fact, A or B?"

"I don't think there can be any doubt about that," Arnold replied.

"I agree with you there. The murder of Saxonby was obviously premeditated, as we know from the preparations made in advance by his murderers. It looks very much as though the forgery and the murder were parts of one and the same conspiracy, as you suggest. And yet, somehow, I don't believe they were. I believe that they were two separate conspiracies, having this in common, that either A or B was concerned in both."

"How do you make that out?"

"I can't quite make it out just yet. But I believe I'm beginning to see a ray of daylight."

Merrion walked over to the inspector's table, upon which the documents mentioned in the report were laid out. "There are a whole lot of points which want explaining," he continued. "Here's one to begin with. The forger was a master of his art. He deceived the bank authorities. You say that Kirby admitted that he could not tell the signature on the forged cheque number 1 from his own. Your experts speak of this signature as an excellent imitation. They say that the handwriting of the body of the cheque closely resembles Kirby's. Yet, apparently, the forger was unable to maintain this standard of excellence. Look at the report. The body of cheque 2 is in a handwriting merely resembling Saxonby's. Whereas the body of cheque 3 is in a handwriting which bears no more than some resemblance to Dredger's. Doesn't that strike you as peculiar?"

"Not necessarily," Arnold replied. "The forger was better acquainted with Kirby's writing than with either of the others."

"Yet he was on such confidential relations with Saxonby that he could get hold of cheques signed by him. No, I believe this falling off in skill was deliberate. Take his attempt at copying Dredger's hand, for instance. If you compare the false with the true, you'll see that it doesn't need an expert to point out that it is a very poor attempt indeed. I think I could undertake to do as well myself."

"It didn't matter much, for the bank people were not familiar with Dredger's writing."

"No. But the forgery was bound to be detected sooner or later. Then, as has actually happened, the handwritings would be compared. That test alone would be sufficient to exonerate Dredger. On the other hand, everything possible seems to have been done to implicate him in the murder. That's one reason why I think that the forgery and the murder were two separate conspiracies. The forgers merely made incidental use of Dredger's name. He had been a confidential employee of Saxonby's, and it would cause no surprise if he were to employ him again when he required a trusted intermediary. But the murderers, as everything shows, have done their best to make him their scapegoat. Look here, let's try to think what would have happened if Saxonby hadn't been murdered."

"It would have made things a lot easier for us. He would have been certain to discover the trick within a day or two. He would have declared that he had not authorised the filling in of cheques 2 or 3, or the writing of the letter of introduction. And he could have told us who might have stolen the signed cheques and notepaper. That may have been one reason why he was murdered."

"It may have been. But let's suppose for a moment that you are Sir Wilfred Saxonby, alive and well after the discovery of the forgery, and that I am Inspector Arnold, seeking information from him. I have still a few questions to put. In the first place, when did you learn that Kirby was going abroad on November 9th?"

"I suppose the answer to that is, Kirby announced his intentions to me a week or two ago, when we were lunching together."

"You had quite forgotten your previous resentment against Kirby?"

"Obviously, since recently we have been in the habit of meeting for lunch fairly frequently."

"Do you not consider it peculiar that these events should have taken place at a time when your son, your daughter and your secretary were all out of London, in each case their absence being due to your own suggestion?"

"The forger probably took advantage of their absence to effect his purpose."

"Kirby's absence was also essential to him. In fact, the coincidence of these absences in his favour is remarkable. You were in the City on Tuesday, November 12th, as your niece has informed us. Can you tell me how you occupied your time that day?"

"In my accustomed duties at my office, of course."

"May I point out that it was the day upon which the Malcolm Dredger account was opened at the bank? Now, let me call your attention to the section of the report dealing with cheque 3. Observe the order in which it was written. First, your signature, a day or two before the body of the cheque and the forger's signature. Lastly, the endorsement, hastily blotted as though the forger were pressed for time. I suggest that you must have signed this cheque no later than Tuesday, the 12th?"

"I have already told you that I must have signed it inadvertently, among other blank cheques presented to me for signature."

"Including cheque B, drawn by you in favour of Malcolm Dredger?"

"Yes, I suppose so."

Merrion laughed. "I thought I should lead you into that trap," he said. "You can't have signed 2 and 3 at the same time. The forger had 2 in his possession before he went to the bank. He could not have obtained the form on which 3 is written until the account was opened. You must, then, have signed two separate batches of cheques, one before the forger went to the bank and one afterwards."

"That's quite likely," Arnold replied, in some confusion.

"If so, quite a considerable percentage of your time at the office must have been spent in signing cheques. Let us pass on to the next point. In the case of 1 and 2, the forger endorsed the cheques at the same time as he forged them. He did not do this in the case of 3. Can you suggest the reason?"

"No, and can't see that the fact is of the slightest significance."

"But I can. Now, one last question. Look at these three cheques. You will observe that 3 has been folded in half, while 1 and 2 have not. How do you account for that?"

This last question was too much for Arnold's patience. "Oh, damn it all!" he exclaimed. "Do you think I should have asked Sir Wilfred such a fool question? How could he be expected to account for it?"

"Because he folded the cheque himself. But your imaginary answers have been far too conscientious. Saxonby, had he lived to be questioned, would have pointed out that since his supposed writing of the body of cheque 2 was admittedly a forgery, it followed that his signatures on 2 and 3 were forgeries as well. He would have maintained that the experts were wrong in believing the signatures to be genuine, and we must admit that possibility ourselves.

"Forging a signature is a very much easier business than forging a set of words and figures. In the first case you have an exact copy to work from. A skilful forger would spend hours copying the signature and comparing it with the original until he had satisfied himself that he could reproduce it perfectly. As an additional safeguard, he could use tracing paper to guide him. This would explain the signature being apparently perfect. If Saxonby had chosen to declare that the signatures were forged, even your experts could not disprove the statement. And their bare opinion would not carry much weight against the word of a man like Saxonby. And he would have given the same explanation as Kirby, to account for the forger's possession of cheque 2. His cheque-book, or a form from it, had been stolen."

"I wish I knew what you were driving at, Merrion," said Arnold impatiently. "What you've just told me that Sir Wilfred might have said is quite possibly what actually happened. But in any case a forgery has been committed, and both Sir Wilfred and Kirby swindled out of a lot of money. Whether Sir Wilfred's signatures are forged or genuine is a detail."

"A detail which may prove to be the essential clue, not only to the forgery, but to the murder as well. However, it's getting late, and I'd like to sleep on all this before I discuss it any more. You're going to meet Richard Saxonby at Southampton to-morrow, aren't you?"

"Yes. I want to make certain that he didn't leave America until the end of last week."

"Then you'll have an opportunity of asking him a question to which I should very much like an answer."

"What's that?" asked Arnold suspiciously.

"Ask him where he bought the wallet that he gave his father for a Christmas present."

XIX

AMONG THE FIRST TO BOARD THE *Iberia* WHEN SHE DOCKED at Southampton next morning was Inspector Arnold. He was not for the moment concerned with making the acquaintance of Richard Saxonby. That could wait. He sought out the purser and satisfied himself that Mr. and Mrs. Saxonby had boarded the ship at New York on November 15th.

That established a convincing alibi, as far as they were concerned. He left the ship and went to the customs shed, where he recognised Irene Wardour in conversation with a couple. The man, from his likeness to his father, could be none other than Richard Saxonby. Arnold introduced himself, and the four travelled up to London together in the boat-train. The topic of conversation was naturally Sir Wilfred's death, and Arnold contrived to remain non-committal. But he contrived tactfully to question Richard Saxonby upon various points. The latter stated emphatically that he had never written to his sister upon the subject of rhododendrons. He had certainly spoken about buying some, probably to several visitors to the house. But he had never given the matter another thought since he had been in America.

On the subject of Dredger he was perfectly frank. "He's a decent old chap, though he's apt to be a bit of a bore at times. He's fond of pottering about in that old car of his, and he comes over to see us sometimes when we're in the country. I asked him to keep an eye on the place now and then while we were away, more because I knew it would please him than for any other reason. Quince is thoroughly to be trusted."

It was not until the train was approaching Waterloo that Arnold had an opportunity of putting Merrion's question. "The wallet?" Richard Saxonby replied. "I don't know where it came from. Torrance could tell you. He and I were talking about what I should give my father, and he suggested a wallet. And next day he had half a dozen sent to the office for me to choose from. I selected one of them and asked him to have my father's initials put on it."

When this reply reached Merrion's ears that afternoon he frowned. "It seems almost impossible to get a definite answer about anything connected with this case," he said. "Now we shall have to ask Torrance where the wallet came from. By the way, I suppose your people are busy tracing the numbers of the notes drawn by the forger from the Bank of Great Britain?"

"Yes, and they have got on to the track of one or two of them already," Arnold replied. "These were exchanged for foreign currency, in notes of which no particulars were taken by the houses where the foreign currency was bought."

"I thought that was probably what had been done with them. Now, shall we go and pay an afternoon call on Torrance? Being Saturday, we're quite likely to find him at home. And I'm really very anxious to know about that wallet."

Arnold allowed himself to be persuaded, and they set out for Maida Vale. Torrance was at home, in the bosom of his family, and insisted upon their having tea. Arnold introduced the subject of the wallet, and Torrance seemed for the moment perplexed. "A wallet bought by Mr. Richard for his father?" he said. "Do you mean the one that you showed me the other day?"

"That appears to be the one," Arnold replied. "I am told that you had a selection sent to the office for Mr. Richard to choose from."

"Oh, yes, I do remember the incident, now you mention it. We had a girl in the office then who came to us from a leather shop in

Cheapside. I asked her if she would mind going round there in her lunch hour and bringing a few wallets back. But the girl has left us now, and I can't remember the name of the shop."

Merrion interposed before Arnold could reply. "Oh, well, it doesn't matter," he said. "Miss Olivia Saxonby's identification of it will be quite sufficient. By the way, there seems to be some doubt as to the time when Sir Wilfred's death became known. When did you first hear of it, for instance?"

"Not until the Friday morning. Miss Olivia rang up the office soon after I got there. About half-past nine, I think it was."

"You didn't by any chance go to the office after you came back from Manchester on Thursday?"

"No, I arrived in London far too late. The place was closed by then. I reached Euston at 8.15, having left Manchester by the 4.20. My wife and a friend of hers met me, and we went into the hotel and had dinner. Miss Olivia might have rung me up here that night, but I don't suppose she knew my address or telephone number. And, in any case, I couldn't have done anything until the morning."

Merrion turned the conversation, and not long afterwards he and Arnold left the house. The inspector seemed puzzled and slightly annoyed. "Why did you drag me all this way to ask a question, and then say it didn't matter?" he demanded.

"Oh, come now!" Merrion replied. "Surely we got all the information we required? There can only be a limited number of leather shops in Cheapside, and it ought not to be beyond the powers of the Yard to trace the purchase of the wallet."

"I don't understand why you're so anxious about that confounded wallet," Arnold grumbled.

"For this reason. I don't believe the wallet given to Saxonby by his son was the one found in his pocket. If it wasn't, then somebody must have procured one exactly like it. And it's ten to one they went to the shop where the original came from. And the shop will remember this second purchase, because of the initials which had to be put on the wallet. So if I were you, I'd get a chap on the job first thing on Monday morning. Meanwhile, you and I are going up to Manchester to-morrow evening."

"To Manchester!" Arnold exclaimed. "Whatever for?"

Merrion smiled. "You've got a very short memory," he replied. "Have you forgotten already that Dredger was the manager for Wigland and Bunthorne in that salubrious city? Don't you think it would be worth while to make a few inquiries on the spot as to his activities before his retirement?"

"And what about this forgery case that I'm supposed to be investigating?"

"Oh, that! That's a very sticky business, and if I were you, I'd handle it pretty carefully. It wouldn't surprise me if, when the facts were known, some way were found of satisfying the aggrieved parties. In any case, the murder of Saxonby seems to me of greater importance."

Arnold allowed himself to be persuaded, and they went to Manchester together on Sunday night. On the following morning they called at the offices of Wigland and Bunthorne, where they were received by the manager who had replaced Mr. Dredger, and who, as it turned out, had been the latter's assistant for many years.

It had been arranged that Merrion should lead the conversation. He made several inquiries about Dredger's habits and peculiarities, without eliciting anything which Arnold did not already know. And then, for no apparent reason, he changed the subject. "You had Mr. Torrance here, the week before last, hadn't you?" he asked.

"Yes, he paid us one of his occasional visits," the manager replied. "He came up from London during Tuesday night, spent the whole of Wednesday and Thursday morning here, and went back that afternoon."

"When did you last see him?"

"He left me about half-past one on Thursday. He said he was going to call on one or two people in Manchester whom he knew, and then catch the 4.20. I remember he said that he would have to be careful not to miss it, as his wife was meeting him at Euston."

Merrion's curiosity seemed to be satisfied. After a few more words, he and Arnold left the office. Once outside, he laughed rather bitterly. "Sorry, but my bright idea hasn't exactly come off," he said. "It couldn't have been done in the time."

"I haven't the remotest idea what you're talking about," Arnold replied.

"Perhaps it's just as well. I'd rather keep my failures to myself."

They walked on for a short distance in silence. And then suddenly Merrion gripped Arnold by the arm. "Good heavens, man, look at that!" he exclaimed.

"Steady on!" replied the inspector resentfully. "You've got infernally powerful fingers. Look at what?"

"Why, that poster, right in front of you. 'Time is Money! Save Time and travel by Air!' I'm getting out of date, that's what's the matter with me. Here, come along!"

He hailed a taxi, and bundled the protesting Arnold into it. "Drive to the aerodrome," he said.

He refused to give any explanation of his conduct. But, on arrival at the aerodrome, he began to make rapid inquiries. As a result of these, he discovered that there was a daily air-service, leaving Manchester at 2 p.m. and arriving at Croydon at 3.45 p.m.

"Now it's up to you," he said to Arnold. "Ask to see the passenger list for Thursday, November 14th."

Thus prompted, Arnold did so. He found that there had been

four passengers that day. Three of these were known to the officials at the aerodrome, as regular passengers. The fourth, who had given the name of Jones, was unknown to them. They could hardly be expected to remember his appearance.

"Then we shall have to pick up the trail at the other end," said Merrion, nothing daunted. "And we may as well fly there, now we're here."

They reached the Croydon airport, and resumed their inquiries. And here they met with a stroke of luck. One of the officials of the company remembered the incident of Mr. Jones, though he was unable to describe him. The reason for his recollection was this. The company provided motor transport for their passengers from the airport to the centre of London. Mr. Jones had not taken advantage of this.

A tedious questioning of those employed at the airport followed. But at last they found a man who carried the story of Mr. Jones a step further. He had been employed in the car-park on the afternoon of November 14th. A chauffeur had driven in, and said that he was expecting the arrival of a passenger. Soon after the plane from Manchester had landed a gentleman had gone up to the car and spoken to the chauffeur. A few minutes later, the gentleman had driven away in the car, leaving the chauffeur behind. The latter had gone off, and the witness had not seen him or the car again.

"Good enough!" said Merrion. "What about getting something to eat, Arnold? Then we'll go back to the Yard, and try to unravel the mystery together."

A couple of hours later they were seated in the inspector's room. Merrion lighted a cigarette and smiled. "Well, have you tumbled to it yet?" he asked.

"You think that this Mr. Jones was Torrance," Arnold replied. "But I don't see how you're going to prove it."

"It's not my job to prove things. That's up to you. All I can do for you is to use my imagination and that's what I've done.

"Ever since we agreed that two men were concerned in Saxonby's murder, I have been convinced that the identity of the one we called B was the clue to the mystery. A was the actual murderer, no doubt, but he might have been anybody, employed by B for the purpose. We had no clue whatever to his identity, and the task of tracing him was hopeless from the first. But B must have been somebody intimately acquainted with Saxonby, and the search for him was therefore limited.

"I have no doubt that we both had Torrance in our minds, as fulfilling this condition. But on consideration, Torrance seemed to be ruled out. He answered all your questions with such obliging readiness that you came to be indebted to him for a large part of your information. I won't stop to point out how cleverly he threw dust in your eyes from the first moment that you saw him. But I must remind you that he was the first person to mention the unlucky Dredger.

"Apart from his willingness to help you, there were two factors which relieved Torrance from suspicion. He was in Manchester, or on his way back from thence, when the crime was committed. Besides, what possible motive had he for desiring Saxonby's death? He gained a small legacy, but that would barely cover the elaborate preparations made for the murder. And his accomplice would certainly demand a share of the profits.

"As you know, the motive of the murder bewildered us both. It seemed to me that only two explanations were possible. Saxonby had been murdered at the instance of some person who would benefit largely by his death. Of these there were three, his son, his daughter, and his niece. Your inquiries made it very difficult to understand how any one of these three could have been implicated. Personally, I inclined to the alternative theory, that Saxonby was murdered for the sake of some valuable object in his possession at the time. I could form no idea of what this valuable object might be. And if I gave any further thought to Torrance this theory seemed definitely to rule him out. He was certainly not at the office on Thursday. How could he know that Saxonby would take something valuable home with him that day?

"There was a fallacy in that argument, though I didn't see it at the time. I puzzled my brains over the nature of that valuable object, and over the arrangements made by Saxonby that all his intimates should be out of the way that day. I got so far as to suspect that Saxonby had been up to something fishy, but I never got within a mile of the truth. It wasn't until last Friday evening, when you told me about the forgery, and showed me the exhibits connected with it, that I saw what the object must have been."

"What was it?" Arnold demanded.

"You wouldn't believe me if I told you off-hand. I shall have to come to it by degrees, so that you can follow my reasoning. Let's return to Torrance, for you've a lot of good honest detective work before you in which he is principally concerned.

"You know that from the first I believed that, at the time of Saxonby's murder, his wallet had been taken and another almost exactly similar substituted for it. In order to secure this second wallet, somebody connected with the murder must have been familiar with the first. This had been given to Saxonby by his son, Richard. Obviously Richard must be questioned on this point. But that was impossible until his arrival in England the day before yesterday. Then it appeared that Richard had not bought the wallet himself, but that Torrance had procured it for him. Torrance's account of the matter you heard yourself. Have inquiries been made among the leather-sellers of Cheapside?"

Arnold picked up his telephone and gave a message. A few minutes later one of his subordinates appeared. This man had made personal inquiries at every shop that sold wallets in Cheapside. At none of them could he secure any information. With one accord the shopmen declared that they had never sent a selection of wallets to the offices of Wigland and Bunthorne in Shrubb Court.

"I rather anticipated that," said Merrion, when the subordinate had left the room. "It struck me on Saturday afternoon that Torrance was a bit taken aback by your question. As a rule, his answers are very prompt, but he wanted time to think of that one. He invented a lie to put you off the scent, of course. But I didn't want him to think that we had discovered the interchange of the wallets, and that it was a vital point. That's why I said it didn't matter, and changed the subject.

"He had his alibi all ready. He had arrived at Euston at 8.15, having left Manchester at 4.20, and so could not possibly have had any concern in the murder of Saxonby in Blackdown Tunnel soon after half-past five. He had been met at the station. But did those who met him see him actually step out of the train? I rather expect you will find that they did not.

"Our inquiries in Manchester seemed to prove his innocence. If he had been seen by the manager there at 1.30, he could not have been at the ventilating shaft with the lorry by five o'clock. He had to go first to Richard Saxonby's place to pick it up. The distance from thence to Manchester must be a good two hundred miles. It seemed at first that it could not have been done. I never thought of that confounded air service. It wasn't until the poster stared me in the face that I saw how the dodge was worked.

"I haven't the slightest doubt that Torrance flew back to Croydon as Mr. Jones. He had a car waiting for him there, as we know. It is immaterial whether he keeps a car and chauffeur of his own. Even if he does, he certainly would not have used them on this occasion. I expect he hired the car in advance. It's one of your jobs to make inquiries about that. I don't think there's any difficulty about sketching out his movements after his arrival in Croydon.

"He arrived at the airport at 3.45, and drove away, I should imagine, by four o'clock. It is fourteen miles from the airport to Richard Saxonby's place, and he would get there comfortably in half an hour. He put the car he was using into Richard's garage, and took out the breakdown lorry, which A had deposited there for him. This he drove to the ventilating shaft. After his adventures there, he drove Mrs. Saxonby's car back to the garage, and exchanged it for the one he had used previously. By then it can hardly have been much later than a quarter-past six. He had plenty of time to drive the twenty-five miles odd to London, leave the car with the people he got it from, and take a taxi to Euston, before the arrival of the 8.15. And I'll bet you a pound to a penny that's what he did."

"But what was the idea?" Arnold asked. "Why in the world should he prepare this elaborate scheme to murder his employer?"

"Ah, that's a long story," Merrion replied. "You'll have to listen to a lot of guess-work if you want me to answer that question. And unfortunately a lot of it can never be verified, for the principal actor in the drama is dead."

XX

MERRION SETTLED HIMSELF DOWN IN HIS CHAIR AND LIGHTED another cigarette. "We've got to go a long way back to find the origin of the trouble," he said. "Back to that unfortunate disagreement between Saxonby and Kirby. We've only heard one side of that story. Saxonby may have had a genuine grievance. In any case, he believed he had. He quarrelled with Kirby, and the two became enemies.

"Now, we've heard enough about Saxonby from various sources to form a fairly accurate estimate of his character. He doesn't sound to me the sort of man who would readily bury the hatchet. But in this case we are told that he made the first advances towards reconciliation, and when these were accepted became once more friendly with his enemy. To such an extent that he took to lunching with him, and even suggested some sort of business co-operation."

"I thought Kirby's story sounded a bit queer, when I heard it," said Arnold.

"I've no doubt it was true, for all that. What was not true was the genuineness of the reconciliation. Saxonby pretended to be reconciled to his enemy for a definite purpose. For years he had been brooding over his grievance. And at last he decided to get his own back on Kirby by attacking his pocket.

"His scheme was a brilliant one, if only he could find the necessary instrument with which to carry it out. He wanted a thoroughly capable forger, who was also capable of carrying out one or two simple burglaries, and I have no doubt that he was ready to pay handsomely for his services. And he found him. How, I don't know.

One can hardly advertise for a person with those particular qualifications. But I shouldn't be at all surprised to learn that Torrance had something to do with it. In any case, I fancy that he took Torrance into his confidence.

"You've got to look at the matter from Saxonby's point of view. He was, we know, a man of very strong opinions. He believed that Kirby had played him a dirty trick. Perhaps he had. Saxonby had had recourse to the usual forms of justice, and failed to obtain redress. It remained to him to pay Kirby back in his own coin. In his eyes, he was not going to commit a crime. He was going to fine Kirby twenty-five thousand pounds. As a magistrate he had probably considered the exact figure of the punishment and fixed it at that. I feel sure that had he lived to collect the money, he would not have applied it to his own purposes. In all probability, he would have handed it on to some charity."

Arnold could no longer restrain his incredulity. "You don't mean to say that Sir Wilfred deliberately signed those cheques, knowing the use to which they would be put?" he exclaimed.

"I do, indeed. It seems to me the only rational explanation of what followed. Saxonby hinted to Kirby of some scheme of business co-operation between them. He repeated these hints to the bank manager. Why? To prepare the way, so that Mr. Harrison would not be surprised when the forger presented the two cheques and the letter of introduction.

"We have no proof of the events which followed. But we have certain indications to guide us, and these I will point out as I go along. Saxonby's plan was simple and ingenious. It was this. To open an account which should be under his control. To pay into this a genuine cheque of his own and a forged cheque of Kirby's, and then to draw out the bulk of the account. In this way he deprived, or hoped to deprive, Kirby of a large sum of money.

"It was essential to his scheme that Kirby should be abroad at the time. His re-established friendship with him gave him an opportunity of learning Kirby's movements in advance. As soon as Saxonby learnt that he would be leaving England on the 9th, he took steps to ensure that his son and daughter should be out of the way. It would never do for them to suspect anything. And he warned his associates, who were, I feel pretty sure, Torrance and the forger, to be ready. As for the forger, I have very little doubt that he was Yates, alias Figgis.

"No doubt Saxonby, in the course of conversation, had learnt from Kirby that he was in the habit of leaving his cheque-book in his desk when he went abroad. Yates' first job was to secure this. Saxonby had provided him with specimens of Kirby's writing and of his signature. Also, incidentally, of his own and Dredger's. Yates set to work and forged cheques 1 and 2, the latter on a form provided by Saxonby for the purpose.

"You will remember that Saxonby was in the City on Tuesday the 12th. No doubt he met Yates that day. Not at his office, but in some quiet spot where they could transact their business. Saxonby inspected the cheques, signed number 2, and gave them back to Yates with the letter of introduction.

"Now that letter is a very interesting document. It is signed by both Saxonby and his daughter. That suggests that it was typed on one of the sheets signed by Mrs. Wardour before she went abroad. The typing was in all probability done by Torrance. It is quite likely, I think, that he told Saxonby that he had spoilt one sheet, and asked for another.

"A second point about the letter is this. The Malcolm Dredger account could only be drawn upon with two signatures. This condition fulfilled a double purpose. It was an additional suggestion of the genuineness of the account. And it was intended as a safeguard against possible treachery on the part of Yates. If only the Malcolm

Dredger signature had been required, Yates might have prepared a cheque for himself, drawn it, and disappeared. But the necessity for two signatures prevented this. He could not have forged Kirby's signature on a cheque supplied to him later than the 9th, for the bank knew that Kirby had gone abroad that day."

"He might have forged Sir Wilfred's signature," Arnold suggested.

"He might have, if he were capable of doing so. But, if your experts are right, he had not done so previously, and he may not have cared to take the risk. I expect that Saxonby took precautions. He may have taken care that Yates should not have access to his signature. And that is why he signed cheques 2 and 3 himself. To make matters quite sure, Yates was instructed to bring the cheque-book to Saxonby as soon as he received it. That, I think, is when Saxonby signed cheque 3.

"We now come to Thursday the 14th, and Yates visit to the office. The purpose of his call was to fill in cheque 3 and attach the Malcolm Dredger signature. The cheque was, I expect, to have been presented that day. But Yates was late. There was no time left to present it and change the notes into foreign currency. So Saxonby allows him to fill up the cheque and sign it, but not to endorse it. It is arranged that Saxonby shall come up to London the following day, that Yates shall meet him there, and endorse the cheque. Meanwhile it will be safest in Saxonby's keeping. He folds it in half, and puts it in his wallet.

"Yates, no doubt, has some satisfactory story to account for being late. Also, he pleads lack of funds. Will Saxonby give him something on account? Saxonby agrees, and gives him the three five-pound notes which he had drawn that morning. They part, having appointed a meeting for the following day.

"I have already tried to give you an idea of the line which Saxonby would have taken when the forgery was discovered. He would have denied all knowledge of the affair. His case was exactly parallel with that of Kirby. If Kirby had been defrauded, so had he. Whatever the experts might say, his signatures were certainly not genuine. His cheque-book, and the sheets of paper signed by Mrs. Wardour, had been stolen from Mavis Court. Somebody must have overheard his preliminary hints to Kirby, and determined to profit by them.

"We must give Saxonby credit for a desire to shield others as well as himself. The forgery carried with it no clue to the complicity of either Torrance or Yates. As for the use of Dredger's name and personality, there was no great harm in that. Dredger could clear himself without difficulty. He could probably prove that he had not visited the bank on either occasion. Besides, care was taken that the false signature and handwriting should not be too accurate copies of the genuine. You would have been sorely puzzled, my friend, if you had had to unravel the plot as Saxonby intended that it should be carried out.

"But Fate, in the shape of Torrance and Yates, intervened. They could not bear to see all this good money go to waste. No doubt they would have been rewarded, after Saxonby had recouped himself for his outlay. But why should they be content with this? If they could obtain cheque 3, and cash it for themselves, they would secure the whole of the profits, instead of a small share.

"The idea, I expect, was Torrance's, and the engineering of the scheme was certainly his. The first problem was how to secure the cheque. Saxonby had obviously worked out his time-table in advance. It was to be completed by Yates and presented on the 14th. But if Yates were to delay his appointment until it was too late to present the cheque that day, what would happen? Saxonby would certainly not allow such a compromising document to leave his possession. He would take it down to Mavis Court and bring it up again in the morning. And he would carry it where he always carried such things, in his wallet.

"He must, then, be murdered while he was carrying it. The tunnel dodge was a brilliant inspiration on Torrance's part. It provided an excellent means of disguising a murder as a suicide. But his powers of invention did not stop there. He had heard of Major Wardour's pistol, either from Mrs. Wardour or from Saxonby. Wardour's possession of that lethal weapon seems to have been pretty widely discussed. Yates, under Saxonby's instructions, was to steal Kirby's cheque-book. Why should he not, under Torrance's, steal the pistol?"

"What about the cartridges which I found in Sir Wilfred's filing cabinet?" Arnold asked.

"Torrance put them there, no doubt, as soon as he arrived at the office on Friday morning. You found the cabinet unlocked. We have only Torrance's word for it that it was usually kept locked. It may not have been, or Torrance may have had a duplicate key. The cartridges were put there for you to find, in order to strengthen your theory of suicide.

"But Torrance was not relying on that alone. Something might go wrong. Some point might crop up in the investigation which would arouse suspicion. It did. You were puzzled at not finding Saxonby's ticket, a small point which Torrance had overlooked. To guard against accidents like this, a second line of defence was necessary.

"Torrance must have realised that it already existed. Saxonby had arranged that Yates should impersonate Dredger for the purposes of the forgery. Why should he not continue to impersonate him for the purposes of the murder? In fact, I expect it was this impersonation which suggested the tunnel. Dredger lived so conveniently close!

"We have already agreed how the murder was committed. There may be a few points connected with it which want clearing up. The letter to Quince, for instance. Torrance typed that, I have no doubt. He used for the purpose the sheet signed by Mrs Wardour which I imagine him to have said he had spoilt. Or Saxonby may have handed over to him the whole half-dozen sheets, which is just as likely. The purloining of the key of Richard Saxonby's garage would present no difficulties. Yates, I have no doubt, is perfectly capable of opening an ordinary back-door with a skeleton key.

"You may be pretty certain of this. We have solved the mystery of the identities of A and B. A was Yates, and B was Torrance. And when Torrance hauled Yates out of the tunnel, the latter had Saxonby's wallet in his pocket. In the wallet was cheque 3, which Yates endorsed subsequently and cashed next morning, as soon as the bank opened. There's rather an interesting point about that, by the way. Torrance admits that Miss Olivia telephoned him the news of her uncle's death about half-past nine on Friday morning. He did not inform the bank until eleven. Obviously to give Yates time to present the cheque and get away with the loot. Now, don't you admit that I've solved your problem for you?"

"Solved the problem!" Arnold exclaimed. "You've made out a very convincing theory, I'll admit that. But you haven't produced a particle of proof in support of it."

"I know that," replied Merrion quietly. "I warned you before I started that I had no proof. You've got to dig away and find that for yourself. And at least I've suggested a dozen likely directions in which to dig. Concentrate upon Torrance. Watch him like a cat. Trace his every action for the last six months, and particularly for the last few days. If you stick to him, you're bound to unearth something. But there's one thing you ought to do without delay."

"What's that?" Arnold asked.

"Release the unfortunate Dredger, and restore him to his sorrowing daughter-in-law. And while you're at it beg his pardon and ask him when and where he last saw Torrance."

XXI

ARNOLD ACTED UPON MERRION'S SUGGESTION. DREDGER WAS released, indignant, but too thankful to regain his liberty to be troublesome. And in reply to the inspector's question he gave a significant account of his last interview with Torrance.

It had taken place on Sunday the 10th. Dredger, following his usual practice, had gone to church, taking his daughter-in-law with him. On their return home they found Torrance awaiting them. He explained that he had just run down to Blackdown to see how Dredger was getting on after his illness. Pressed to stay to lunch, he had refused, saying that he had an appointment in London. The maid said later that Torrance had arrived half an hour before the return of the Dredgers from church. On her telling him where they were, he said he would wait, and she had shown him into the sitting-room. She had distinctly heard the sound of the typewriter while he was there.

This was certainly a point in favour of Merrion's theory. It explained how the letter to Quince might have been typed on Dredger's machine. Arnold made a note of this, and proceeded with his inquiries.

His next discovery was even more significant. Cautious inquiries in Maida Vale revealed the fact that Torrance did not possess a car of his own. He was in the habit of hiring one, as he required it, and driving it himself. The firm which supplied the cars was located. Reference to their books showed that Torrance had hired a car from them on Thursday the 14th. On the previous Tuesday he had rung up and given his instructions. These were that the car was to meet him at Croydon airport at half-past three on the 14th. The car had been sent, and shortly before four o'clock Torrance had taken the car over from the driver, who had returned to London by bus. Torrance had returned the car in person just before half-past seven.

Inquiries throughout the City at last brought news of the wallet. The manager of a shop in Bishopsgate had the following story to tell. One day before Christmas a messenger had come to him from Wigland and Bunthorne, bearing a note as evidence of good faith. This note had for some reason been kept. It was typed upon the firm's notepaper, and signed "Henry Torrance." A selection of wallets had been given to the messenger. These had been returned later in the day, with a verbal message indicating the one chosen, and asking that the initials W.S. in gold should be placed upon it. This was done. The wallet had been delivered to the offices of Wigland and Bunthorne, and duly paid for.

Some time during October, a gentleman, whose description might well have applied to Torrance, called at the shop. He purchased a wallet exactly similar to the one previously supplied to Wigland and Bunthorne. He gave his name as William Smith, and asked that his initials, W.S., should be placed on the wallet in gold. A couple of days later he collected the wallet and paid for it. The manager had remarked to one of his assistants that it was curious that two exactly similar wallets should have been supplied to people with the same initials.

Arnold was elated at this discovery. Whether or not Torrance had been the purchaser of the second wallet, he had lied about the origin of the first. This, of itself, was suggestive of his guilt.

The inspector took an early opportunity of interviewing Richard Saxonby. He learnt that Torrance was a frequent visitor to his house in the country. Richard distinctly remembered talking to him about his project of planting the bed opposite the front door with rhododendrons. He had certainly mentioned the matter to many other people as well, including Dredger.

In the course of this conversation it transpired that the key of the back door of Richard's house had been lost, shortly before his departure to America. The lock had not been changed, but a new key had been fitted by the local ironmonger. Its loss had been noticed in the evening, when it was time to lock up the house. Questioned by Arnold, Richard expressed a certainty that Torrance had been to the house that day.

The letter introducing the false Malcolm Dredger to the bank was submitted to experts upon typewriters. They declared that the typing of it corresponded exactly with that of one of the specimens supplied to Arnold by Torrance. The particular machine from which the specimen had been obtained was, upon investigation, found in Torrance's room at Shrubb Court.

Soon after Arnold had gathered this scattered information, he met Merrion once more and passed it on to him. "I've learnt enough now to convince me that your theory is correct," he said. "But I daren't arrest Torrance on the evidence I've got. The case against him wouldn't convince a jury. And I can't find the slightest trace of the other fellow. Though I believe I've got a hint as to who he is."

"That's something," Merrion replied. "What have you heard?"

"I've been talking to Dredger again. He bears me no grudge, and we get on capitally now. I let him talk, and on one occasion I picked up this story.

"About two years ago, while Dredger was still manager of the Manchester office, a sudden pressure of work made it necessary for him to take on a couple of extra clerks. One of these was a young chap called Whittaker. Dredger took to him at once. He was a smart, bright lad, and said he had been an actor, but gave it up as he could not get enough engagements to keep him properly."

"That sounds promising," Merrion remarked.

"Wait a minute. Dredger was so impressed with his abilities that he kept him on, even after the rush had abated. All went well for some time. Then it was discovered that somebody had been forging Dredger's name. It was nothing really serious, since only small sums were involved. The matter was traced to Whittaker, and the facts reported to the head office. Dredger offered to make good the deficiencies, and Sir Wilfred declined to prosecute."

"I wonder if he had an idea, even then, that he might some day require the services of a forger? What became of Whittaker?"

"He was, of course, dismissed. But Dredger, who seems to be of a forgiving disposition, kept in touch with him. He came up to London, and somehow managed to earn a living for himself. Now, listen to this. Some three or four months ago Dredger was asked by Sir Wilfred if he happened to know Whittaker's address."

Merrion whistled softly. "The devil he was!" he exclaimed.

"Dredger gave it to him, of course, without troubling his head to ask what he wanted it for. Naturally, I too asked for that address, and got on to the job. I found myself at a cheap and shabby boarding-house, but the bird had flown. He hadn't been seen since the morning of Wednesday the 13th, which you will remember, was the day that the breakdown lorry was driven from Plymouth.

"Of course, I made inquiries, but nobody could tell me much about Whittaker. He seemed to have no definite employment, but came and went irregularly. Latterly he seemed to have money to spend. He gave out that some friends of his were going to start him in a garage near London. And it was known that he spent a day in Plymouth during October, that was when he bought the lorry."

"He's your man," said Merrion confidently. "Everything dovetails in to perfection. He could impersonate Dredger, having had the opportunity of studying him at first hand. But where he may be by this time, heaven only knows."

All this while, Scotland Yard was unobtrusively keeping a sharp eye on Torrance's movements. A day or two after his conversation with Merrion, it came to Arnold's ears that Torrance and his family proposed to spend a week in Brighton, during which period his flat in Maida Vale would be shut up. This aroused his suspicions, and the watch upon the flat was redoubled.

On the third evening after it had been left unoccupied, one of the watchers saw a man, who seemed to resemble Torrance, enter the building. He immediately communicated with Arnold, who arrived on the scene without delay.

It was a dark, unpleasant evening, and for some time Arnold and his companion watched the flat without incident. At last a second figure approached, that of a young man. He too entered the building. A few moments later a light appeared behind the drawn curtains of one of the rooms of the flat.

Arnold curbed his impatience, and waited for perhaps five minutes later. Then, swiftly, he and his companion ran into the block and charged up the stairs. There was no standing upon ceremony. Arnold flung himself at the door of the flat, which burst open under the impact. There was a startled shout from within, and that led him into the room where the light was burning. Two men confronted him. One was Torrance. The other was a tall, well-dressed good-looking young man. On a table between them were laid several neat bundles of foreign notes.

The inspector wasted no time in unnecessary argument. He took them both to the police-station, where he charged them both with being concerned in the forgery of Kirby's signature to a cheque. Next day they appeared before the magistrate and were remanded in custody.

Then began a most instructive series of identifications.

The young man was identified by the keeper of the boarding-house, by his wife, by the servant, and independently by Dredger, as Whittaker.

He was identified by the manager of the Celtic Garage at Plymouth, and also by the morose Bleak, as Figgis.

Finally, he was identified by three members of the staff of Wigland and Bunthorne as Sir Wilfred Saxonby's visitor, who had given the name of Yates.

Arnold felt that his case was now complete. He charged both prisoners with the wilful murder of Sir Wilfred Saxonby.

At this Torrance, who had faced the charge of forgery with confidence, completely broke down. He seemed to think that he could save his own skin by betraying his companion, who had actually fired the fatal shot. He made a full statement, very damaging to himself, since it showed that the idea of murdering Saxonby was his alone. It was only reluctantly that Whittaker had been induced to participate in it.

His statement coincided almost exactly with Merrion's reconstruction. But it contained one rather curious point, concerning the pistol. It had first been arranged that Saxonby should be stabbed, with a hunting-knife which he was known to possess, and which Whittaker was to steal from Mavis Court. And then occurred a curious incident, of which Torrance saw how to take full advantage.

He had from the first been in Saxonby's confidence regarding the scheme for revenge upon Kirby. And one day Saxonby asked him if he thought that Whittaker could be trusted on a delicate mission. Torrance had replied that he thought so, if it was made worth his while. And then Saxonby told him about Wardour's pistol. Mrs. Wardour was nervous about it, and Saxonby himself shared her fears. You never could tell what a man like that might do in a fit of temper.

If the pistol should happen to be stolen while Wardour was in France, it would be a capital thing for everybody concerned.

So Whittaker was entrusted with the job, which he carried out successfully. He conveyed the pistol to Torrance, who showed it to Saxonby, and then retained it on the pretext that he would find a means of disposing of it. He had immediately seen the one to which could be put a pistol with the initials S.W. upon it. As for the cartridges found in the cabinet, that was explained by the fact that Torrance possessed a duplicate key.

The trial created a great sensation. Torrance, in spite of his confession, pleaded not guilty, a course which was followed by Whittaker. The defence made a great point of the fact that the evidence was purely circumstantial. There was no proof that either of the prisoners was on or near the scene of the crime at the time the murder was committed.

But this argument failed to convince the jury. Both prisoners were found guilty, and sentenced to death.

They were duly hanged.

THE END

Also Available

THE SECRET OF HIGH ELDERSHAM

"They're terrible mistrustful of strangers in these parts."

Samuel Whitehead, the new landlord of the Rose and Crown, is a stranger in the lonely East Anglian village of High Eldersham. When the newcomer is stabbed to death in his pub, and Scotland Yard are called to the scene, it seems that the veil dividing High Eldersham from the outside world is about to be lifted.

Detective-Inspector Young forms a theory about the case so utterly impossible that merely entertaining the suspicion makes him doubt his own sanity. Surrounded by sinister forces beyond his understanding, and in need of rational assurance, he calls on a brilliant amateur and 'living encyclopedia', Desmond Merrion. Soon Merrion falls for the charms of a young woman in the village, Mavis Owerton. But does Mavis know more about the secrets of the village than she is willing to admit?